Instinct was urging Adam to hustle her straight back into the lift and have her escorted off the premises because as he approached her it was becoming appallingly apparent that her effect on him was as immediate and intense as he recalled.

A month ago, she'd decimated fourteen years of steely control with one blink of her beautiful brown eyes and he was in danger of allowing her to do it again now.

No. He could handle the attraction, he assured himself as he came to a stop in front of her and banked the response of his body to her intoxicating proximity. It wouldn't be the first time he'd denied his libido. Once this job was underway, he would keep interaction to a minimum and maintain his distance unless strictly necessary. He had no reason to deliberately seek her out and more than enough work to be getting on with. He would focus on the endgame and keep a clear head. It was only for two weeks. It would pass in a flash.

"Adam Courtney, CEO," he said, pasting a professional smile to his face and h...

hand. "Welcome to t...

Billion-Dollar Bet

*Three rival billionaires... Two huge problems...
One bet to solve them both!*

Zane deMarco, Adam Courtney and Cade Landry
have two problems:

1. In their individual and ruthless pursuit of a failing
company, they're pushing the share price sky-high.

2. The billionaire playboys are being scandalously
called out online for their dating habits.

There's only one way to solve both... Whoever can
stay a one-woman man for the entire summer will
not only rid themselves of the rumors but add a new
company to their business portfolio.

They have a lot to lose, but a lot to gain. And what's
betting all of them also find passion worth risking it
all for?

Read Zane's story in:

Billion-Dollar Dating Game by Natalie Anderson

And enjoy Adam's story:

Boss with Benefits by Lucy King

Both available now!

And look out for Cade's story:

After-Party Consequences by Heidi Rice

Coming soon!

BOSS WITH BENEFITS

LUCY KING

Harlequin

PRESENTS

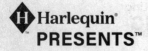

Harlequin® PRESENTS™

ISBN-13: 978-1-335-93919-7

Boss with Benefits

Copyright © 2024 by Lucy King

Harlequin Enterprises ULC
22 Adelaide St. West, 41st Floor
Toronto, Ontario M5H 4E3, Canada
www.Harlequin.com

Printed in Lithuania

Recycling programs for this product may not exist in your area.

MIX
Paper | Supporting responsible forestry
FSC® C021394
www.fsc.org

Lucy King spent her adolescence lost in the glamorous and exciting world of Harlequin when she really ought to have been paying attention to her teachers. But as she couldn't live in a dreamworld forever, she eventually acquired a degree in languages and an eclectic collection of jobs. After a decade in southwest Spain, Lucy now lives with her young family in Wiltshire, England. When not writing or trying to think up new and innovative things to do with mince, she spends her time reading, failing to finish cryptic crosswords and dreaming of the golden beaches of Andalucia.

Books by Lucy King

Harlequin Presents

Stranded with My Forbidden Billionaire

Passion in Paradise

A Scandal Made in London

Lost Sons of Argentina

The Secrets She Must Tell
Invitation from the Venetian Billionaire
The Billionaire without Rules

Passionately Ever After...

Undone by Her Ultra-Rich Boss

Heirs to a Greek Empire

Virgin's Night with the Greek
A Christmas Consequence for the Greek
The Flaw in His Rio Revenge

Visit the Author Profile page
at Harlequin.com for more titles.

For Heidi and Natalie, my fellow billionaire bachelor bet babes.

CHAPTER ONE

'Do I know you? Because you look a lot like my next girlfriend.'

Sitting at the bar of Manhattan's newest and buzziest cocktail lounge, Ella Green winced. The chat-up line delivered by the guy on her left was as repellent as the malodorous combination of alcohol, sweat and cologne that was emanating from him and catching her at the back of her throat. It was the twenty-first century. Could a woman *still* not drown her sorrows in public on her own on a Friday night in June in peace?

'You don't know me, I'm afraid,' she said politely, as she ramped up the *back off* vibes and edged away.

'But I'd like to,' said the guy, leaning a little more heavily on the bar, his smile presumably aiming for seductive but resulting in somewhere between dribbling and lecherous. 'I'm Pete. Do you have a name or should I just call you "mine"?'

Ugh. 'Never do that.'

'You know, if I could rearrange the alphabet, I'd put "U" and "I" together.'

Ella sighed. 'It's "you" and "me."'

'What?'

'If you're going to try and pick me up with terrible lines, at least be grammatically correct about it.'

Utter befuddlement met that remark. '"U" and "me" doesn't work,' said Pete with a frown.

'Well, there you go then. Take the hint.'

He didn't. Instead, he doubled down. 'Would you at least stroke my arm so I can tell my friends I've been touched by an angel?'

'No.'

'Then how about I stroke yours?'

He reached out and put his hand on her bare upper arm, and in the blink of an eye she'd spun round, her knee had connected with his groin and the contents of her glass had landed on his shirt.

Pete gave a yowl and clutched his genitals, his face contorted in pain, but Ella refused to feel guilty. She had given him every opportunity to go away and leave her alone. It was his own fault he hadn't taken it.

'Sorry,' she said, not sorry at all. 'Dodgy stool.'

Gasping and spluttering, Pete plucked at the vodka-soaked cotton, puce with humiliation and evidently furious. 'Frigid bitch.'

'Inebriated jerk.'

With a filthy glare, he limped off and Ella swung back to the bar. She wasn't frigid. Or a bitch. She just valued her personal space and didn't appreciate being groped against her will. Like most people, she imagined. Although most people probably hadn't grown up in a dangerous, deprived backwater of a neighbourhood where it was sensible to learn self-defence at an early age.

'Nice moves.'

This dry remark came from the guy on her right, who was a different kettle of fish entirely.

She'd been bitterly contemplating her drink when he'd sat down beside her ten minutes earlier. An odd sort of charge had electrified the displaced air. An exquisitely woodsy scent had wafted towards her. Her skin prickling in the most peculiar way, she'd instinctively glanced over and out of habit had catalogued what she'd been able to see from the side.

A man of around her age, maybe a few years older. Thick dark hair. Straight nose. Square jaw with the hint of a five-o'clock shadow. Pale blue Oxford shirt, sleeves rolled up. Tanned, muscled forearms. An expensive-looking gold-faced and tan-leather-strapped watch on his left wrist. Big hands, long fingers, short, neat nails.

Very attractive in profile, she'd concluded as a hot shiver had rippled down her spine. Possibly even more so from the front.

She'd reluctantly averted her gaze before he could catch her ogling. He'd summoned the bartender and given the order for a large Scotch, his cut glass accent indicating that he came from the other side of the Atlantic. Parking her curiosity and leaving him to whatever had him also studying his drink, Ella had resumed her acidic ruminations on the gross unfairness of life that meant her unspeakable ex was up for an industry award while she was still trying to repair her career after their short yet illicit workplace affair blew up a year ago. But she'd nevertheless remained acutely aware of her neighbour's size, stillness and his intriguing sense of contained power—until her attention had been claimed in the other direction.

Now, however, with that deep deliciously sexy voice aimed straight at her, the timbre of it vibrating through her body and igniting her nerve endings, she turned. Her gaze met his, and for one breathtaking moment the world slammed to a halt. The dimly lit bar with its glittering opulence and sultry vibe vanished. The bottom fell out of her stomach. Her heart skipped a beat and then began to race.

She'd been right, she thought dazedly, her head spinning and her temperature rocketing. He *was* even more attractive from the front. His eyes were like the ocean. As blue and as deep as the Pacific. And suddenly she felt a stab of empathy for Pete, because as cringeworthy as the thought was, she wanted to dive right into them.

After what felt like an hour but could only have been a second, Ella blinked, snapping the sizzling connection. Her surroundings swam into focus and the world cranked back into gear.

'I don't know what you mean,' she said, still a little breathless from the impact he was having on her. 'It was an accident.'

His mesmerising eyes glinted with wry amusement. 'Of course it was.'

'The perils of an uneven floor.'

'A dodgy stool, I thought you said.'

'It's a dangerous combination.'

'And there was me deliberating over whether to intervene.'

'How would you have done that?' she asked, immediately envisaging him stripping off his shirt and squaring up to her former admirer, all rippling muscles and simmering outrage on her behalf. Which was bizarre when, firstly, she was a financial auditor with a keen eye for numerical detail but next to no imagination and, secondly, she had never *ever* needed rescuing.

'I hadn't thought that far.'

That was a shame. 'Lucky, then, that I can take care of myself.'

'Not so lucky for Pete.'

'I gave him fair warning.'

'More than enough,' he agreed. 'His lines were appalling. He needs to learn to take no for an answer.' He ran his gaze over her face, her hair, her body, scorching her like a laser where it lingered. Then he added, with the glimmer of a devastating smile, 'But I can't blame him for trying.'

In response to his appreciative scrutiny—*so* much more welcome than the leery Pete's—Ella flushed from head to toe and fizzed with pleasure. 'Thank you. I think.'

'I'm Adam.'

Swinging round, he held out his hand and she automatically took it. 'Ella,' she said, just about able to recall her name even though tiny shocks were shooting up her arm into her head and short-circuiting her brain.

'May I replenish your drink?'

He could do anything he wanted with that voice and those eyes. If he reached out and peeled off her dress, right here, right now, she'd be helpless to stop him. In fact, she'd probably tell him to hurry up. And that was concerning for a single-minded control freak who made decisions with her head, not her heart. But she couldn't remember the last time she'd been so instantly and comprehensively attracted to a man. Ever.

'That's very straightforward of you,' she said, boldly checking out the perfection of his masculine features and the impressive breadth of his shoulders while the heat whipping around inside her coalesced into a puddle of lust that settled low in her abdomen. 'Don't you want to tell me that even though you're not a photographer you can picture us together?'

'No,' he said, his voice dropping an octave. 'Although I can.'

'How?'

'You don't want to know.'

'I do.'

He leaned in and murmured, 'It involves a large bed and no clothes.'

God. He didn't beat about the bush. If she'd had any doubt about the mutuality of the attraction, it had just been pulverised. Her mouth dried. Her entire body throbbed. This man could invade her personal space any day of the week, she thought as she exhaled slowly and swallowed hard. 'Tell me more.'

'I'm still working on the details,' he said, drawing back just enough for her to be able to see that his pupils were so dilated little of the blue remained. 'But if you're after a line, I'm more than happy to admit that I was feeling a little off today until you just turned me on. Perverse, I know, but there it is. You're beautiful and fierce. It's another dangerous combination.'

If anything was dangerous, it was him. She'd always enjoyed this dance, the flirty back and forth and the heavy looks—until the lousy experience with her ex had meant that she'd had to focus on rebuilding her career to the exclusion of all else. But what was going on here was on a whole other level.

This man, who was gazing at her with such heat that she felt as though she could catch fire any moment now, was unleashing that reined-in power she'd sensed earlier. He wasn't bothering with a slow-burning build-up. He was pouring petrol on the bonfire and setting it alight. Deliberately or not, he was killing her brain cells, one by one, and unravelling the control she'd always considered rock solid.

They'd only been talking for five minutes, but already she could visualise them writhing around together in that bed. Her breasts were tingling. White-hot desire was pouring through her with such strength that her inhibitions were fast becoming history. She wanted to leap onto his lap and seal her mouth to his while yanking his shirt aside and putting her hands on his bare chest.

It was insane. Incomprehensible. And to someone who'd had to forswear fun for the last twelve months to concentrate on her career and had sorely missed intimacy of the steamy, sweaty kind, it was absolutely thrilling.

'What were you drinking?'

That was an excellent question. Liquid dopamine? Dynamite? 'Martini.'

'How do you like it?'

'The dirtier the better.'

A faint smile curved his gorgeous mouth and detonated tiny bombs of excitement inside her. 'A woman after my own heart.'

'I'm not after anyone's heart,' she countered with an imperceptible shudder. Never had been, never would be. Even the thought of giving up her hard-won independence brought her out in a cold sweat. Compromise? Sacrifice? No, thank you very much. She'd had to climb countless ladders to get out of the impoverished, fetid and perilous trailer park in which she'd grown up and make something of herself. Conquering the world of auditing was her number one priority and she needed no distractions.

But the pure unadulterated lust currently ravaging her system? That she could indulge.

'Neither am I,' he said with equal intensity.

'Single?'

'Always.'

'You could not be more perfect,' she breathed on a sigh.

'Nor could you.'

For one long hot moment, they just stared at each other, the air between them humming with energy, her drink forgotten. His hand found her bare knee, and her skin first shivered then sizzled when it inched up her thigh. She leaned in as if magnetised and touched her fingers to those of his other hand, which rested on the bar. The buzzing electricity that flowed through the circuit they formed was so powerful she wouldn't be surprised if the effects could be felt in Brooklyn.

His gaze dropped to her mouth and her heart thundered. The desire radiating off him was almost palpable. She'd never experienced such instant and blistering chemistry or felt so...*carnal*.

The sensible, rational voice in her head—to which she usually paid avid attention—insisted that this was no simple flirtation, that she was way out of her depth, that she really should not do what it suspected she was going to do. She must not lose focus, it demanded. Rebuilding her career had been her primary goal for the last twelve months and she had to stick to that.

But it didn't stand a chance.

Nothing mattered except satisfying the primal urge to act on the need rampaging through her. Like a train thundering along the tracks, she was heading in one direction only, her destination flashing at her like a beacon from the moment their gazes had collided. It

wasn't as if she'd be there for long, she assured herself. She'd be back to reality soon enough.

'Would you like to take this conversation somewhere a bit more private?' she said, so desperate to
assuage the throbbing ache between her legs that she
was incapable of thinking about anything else.

He didn't hesitate. He didn't even blink. 'Yes,' he
said, sounding as though he'd swallowed gravel. 'I
very much would.'

What the hell he thought was doing as he closed the
bathroom door behind him and flipped the lock, Adam
Courtney had no idea. He didn't pick women up in
bars, no matter how powerfully sexy and beautiful
they were. He'd given up that sort of selfish, reckless
behaviour fourteen years ago at the age of eighteen,
when his mother had died because he'd been too busy
screwing around to save her, and Charley, his then
eight-year-old sister, had been left rudderless.

At no point since had he relapsed. These days, his
ultra-brief relationships were infrequent and discreet.
He would not turn into his callous, philandering father, he'd reminded himself over the years on the rare
occasion his control threatened to slip. His reputation
for steadiness and integrity was inextricably linked
to that of the Courtney Collection, the luxury goods
empire that had been in his family for over a century
and which he now headed up, and he would do nothing to jeopardise it.

Yet he hadn't hesitated for even a moment when

Ella had suggested he give her a couple of minutes and then join her in here. His reputation hadn't crossed his mind. For the first time in years, he wasn't thinking with his brain. From the moment he'd looked into her gorgeous brown eyes, he'd been driven entirely by the clamouring needs of his body, and he was far too battered by recent events to resist the power of the desire that had surged through him.

He'd noticed her the minute he'd reached the bar at which he'd intended to rid himself of the tension that had been dogging him for weeks by consuming large quantities of single malt. It had been impossible not to. Her hair flowed down her back in long golden waves that gleamed in the low lighting and looked as though they would feel like silk. Her sleeveless dress, the colour of buttermilk, clung to generous curves and revealed toned tanned arms. A brief glance to his left as he'd taken possession of the stool to her right had told him that her profile was exquisite, her complexion flawless. And judging by the looks she'd attracted, he wasn't the only one to think so.

But although his interest had been piqued, he hadn't planned on speaking to her. She'd appeared preoccupied and he'd had plenty else to dwell on. Such as Helberg Holdings, the global conglomerate that had been in his sights for over a decade, which was in serious financial trouble and therefore ripe for a takeover.

The minute he'd heard seven months ago that the cantankerous owner had died, he'd started buying up the dirt-cheap shares, and victory, he'd thought with grim satisfaction as his stake steadily grew, would soon be his. Once in his possession, he'd sell off everything except Montague's, the jewellery business that had been beloved of his mother and used to belong to the Courtney Collection until his father had sold it to Reed Helberg for a dollar out of spite. That, he'd welcome back into the fold and restore to its former glory, and then, perhaps, the crushing guilt that had weighed on him so heavily and for so long might lift a little.

Lately, however, the availability of the stock had plummeted, and the share price was rocketing to a level that was beginning to challenge even his exceedingly deep pockets. He faced the very real possibility that the company could slip through his fingers, and that simply could not happen. Whatever the threat—rivals, internal machinations, *anything*—he needed to neutralise it.

Adam had been contemplating hiring a private investigator to dig into what was going on when the idiotic Pete had made his move and then the coolly magnificent Ella had made hers. He hadn't been able to resist checking she was all right under the guise of expressing his admiration at her handling of the situation, but never in a million years could he have anticipated feeling as though he'd been struck by lightning when their eyes had met.

Yet that was precisely what had happened.

In the space of a millisecond, his pulse rate had shot through the roof and his head had emptied of everything but the need to get her naked. Every drop of his blood had rushed to his groin and the erection he'd sprung had been so hard it had ached.

They'd talked—about what he could hardly recall—and all he'd been able to focus on was her mouth. He'd wanted it on his, on his skin, taking him in as deeply as she could. She'd stared at him hungrily, obliterating years of ironclad control and stripping away millennia of civility, and if she hadn't suggested this, he had no doubt that he would have.

Now she was standing at the black marble-and-gilt vanity unit with her back to him, feet apart, her hands gripping the edges. Her warm brown eyes connected with his in the Art Deco mirror, glittering with excitement and invitation. Any lingering doubt he might have had about the wisdom of what he was about to do was swept away by a thundering tsunami of desire.

'We have to be quick,' she said raggedly, her cheeks flushed, her chest heaving.

'That's not going to be problem.' Thanks to his recent fixation with Helberg Holdings, he hadn't had sex in months and was wound so tightly he was about to explode.

Stepping forwards and pressing up against her, he swept her hair to one side and set his mouth to her neck. Her skin tasted faintly salty. The coconut scent of her shampoo wafted into his head. He briefly thought of the many holidays that gruelling sixteen-hour days hadn't allowed him to take, but then she shivered and moaned, grinding her bottom into his groin, and he stopped thinking about anything at all.

Compelled by the primitive need to be inside her slick welcoming heat, Adam unbuckled his belt and unzipped his trousers. He pushed down the clothing that was in the way and, gritting his teeth, rolled on the condom he'd fished out of his wallet. He wanted to touch her everywhere, slowly and thoroughly, savouring the experience, but that wasn't an option under the circumstances. So he put his hands on her bare upper arms and then ran them down her body, over her soft curves, until he reached the hem of her dress. They shook as he lifted it and stilled completely when he found her naked where he'd expected underwear.

'I thought I'd save some time,' she murmured in response to the hiss of his breath through his teeth.

'I'm impressed,' he said, his blood pumping through his veins even faster as he slid one hand round between her legs, feeling the dampness there, and pressed his fingers to her core. 'I'm way beyond thought.'

Ella groaned and bent forwards, shifting her feet wider apart to allow him better access. 'Hurry,' she breathed unnecessarily, because he was already there, the blunt head of him pushing at her entrance. She gave her bottom a quick wiggle of encouragement—not that he needed it—and with one smooth hard thrust he lodged thickly inside her.

His heart lurched and then began to pound. She swore softly, closed her eyes and threw her head back, her golden hair shimmering in the low light. Bewitched by the sight of it as much as the ferocious desire thundering through him, he was barely aware of his hand gliding up her back and into the glorious tresses as he began to move in and out of her with long steady strokes.

'Yes,' she breathed on a ragged pant, granting him the permission he hadn't even known he was seeking to close his fist around the silky strands close to her scalp and tug on them lightly.

Gasping, instinctively arching her back, she took him in further, the penetration at this angle so deep he saw stars. She opened her eyes and their gazes once again connected in the mirror, with an unexpected intimacy that tightened his chest. But he didn't have the wherewithal to wonder why that should be. His control was fast disintegrating. The exquisite tension inside him was intensifying, the muscles in his stomach, his back and his chest contracting. His fingers were tightening around her hair and his thrusts were quickening.

Her breathing was harsh and the look in her eyes was wild, desperate, and he didn't know how much longer he could hold on, when suddenly she tensed and clapped a hand over her mouth, muffling her cry as she shattered around him. Everything inside him spiralled in, sucking into a single point, a black hole in the pit of his groin. He thrust one last time, hard and deep, and the whole universe collapsed into noth-

ingness before suddenly exploding out the other side
into colour and light.

When feeling eventually returned to his limbs
and his head had stopped spinning, Adam carefully
withdrew and dealt with the condom, his body still
spasming with tiny darts of lingering pleasure. As
he put himself back together and regained control,
Ella slowly straightened, smoothed her dress and her
hair, then turned to face him, flushed, glowing, still
slightly tousled.

'That was...' She shook her head, looking dumb-
struck. 'I don't even know what that was.'

Neither did he. He'd never experienced anything
like it. He usually deployed far more finesse, although
he usually had far more time and these days he favoured a bed. All he *did* know was that he wanted
to take her home and do what they'd just done over
and over again in every position under the sun all
night long—and not just because it would obliterate
thoughts of difficult boards and troubling share prices.
'How about that martini?'

For a moment, she looked torn and his pulse spiked.
But then she gave her head a regretful shake and
picked up her bag.

'Some other time,' she said, hooking the strap onto
her shoulder while a wrecking ball of disappointment
thumped him in the gut. 'But thank you.'

With the faintest of smiles, she dropped a quick kiss
on his cheek as she brushed past him, then unlocked
the door and slipped out.

CHAPTER TWO

Four weeks later

ADAM ARRIVED AT the office at 8:00 a.m. after a Fourth of July holiday weekend that had very much *not* been a holiday. In fact, the last forty-eight hours had been so frustrating and stressful they had given him a full-on tension headache that still nagged at his temples.

The trouble had started bright and early on Saturday, following a round of squash that he'd arranged with Zane deMarco and Cade Landry in response to the report he'd received from the private investigators he'd hired to dig into the Helberg Holdings conundrum.

Zane was a deceptively laid-back corporate raider from the poorer part of the Hamptons, who he knew from his Cambridge rowing days and considered a friend. Cade, a hard-edged lone wolf from Louisiana who'd worked his way up from construction worker to big-shot property developer in just over a decade, he'd become acquainted with since arriving in New York.

The three of them crossed paths at functions and

met up occasionally to shoot the breeze or thrash the living daylights out of each other on the squash court. They were equally driven, equally competitive and had always operated in different spheres of business.

Until now.

Because both men, the report had revealed, were behind the Helberg Holdings share price surge. And neither, Adam had learned to his annoyance when he'd confronted them in the sauna to which they'd headed after the match, was prepared to step aside.

'No can do,' Zane had drawled at the same time as Cade had given his head a sharp shake and declared, 'Not happening. It's a once-in-a-lifetime opportunity, y'all.'

Of course it was, and with hindsight, Adam didn't know why he hadn't considered their involvement sooner. The portfolio of heritage enterprises owned by Reed Helberg was vast and varied, and in business his so-called friends were sharks. But he'd had no time to process the implications of this unbreakable three-way dead lock because Cade had then delivered yet more bad news, the trouble this time brewing in the offices of *Blush*, the women's glamour magazine.

'Did y'all know we're the star players in their latest dumb article?' he'd practically snarled, having just received a text from his PR consultant on the subject. 'The Billionaire Bachelors Least Likely to Marry. Apparently, we three have been tagged as the One-Date Wonders—the guys with the longest odds—and they've already started a tally of how many dates we'll have racked up by Labor Day… My PR team are freaking out about it. Personally, I don't give a damn what a bunch of click-bait junkies and their enablers think of my dating habits. But no way in hell am I letting anyone make me look like a jerk who can't keep his junk in his pants.'

Although he wouldn't have put it in those terms, Adam had shared Cade's sentiment. His integrity was everything, and this article, with both its inaccurate, unsavoury slant and the traction it was gaining, had sounded as though it had reputational damage written all over it. He, the board and the women he was regularly photographed with knew that his dating record wasn't what it seemed—ninety-five percent of them were strategically selected by him to promote the company, and there weren't even that many of them—but of what use was that? The optics were disastrous and the fallout could be catastrophic. At the height of his father's philandering, which by that point had become legally as well as morally questionable and therefore even greater fodder for the merciless tabloids, sales had plummeted by seventy-five percent.

That wasn't happening again on *his* watch, he'd thought, his temperature soaring in a way that had had nothing to do with the heat of the sauna. He'd worked himself to the bone building up both his reputation and that of the Courtney Collection, and he was not having four years of blood, sweat and tears put at risk simply to fill gossipy column inches and collect social media likes.

They'd all agreed that the interest in them needed to be nixed asap. But it was Zane who'd come up with the idea they take themselves off the market by dating one woman—and one woman only—for the duration of the summer.

At the time, that suggestion had made no sense to Adam at all. How on earth would *that* reduce the rampant interest in them? he'd asked himself while wondering whether the ruthless corporate raider had actually lost his mind. Wouldn't the sudden shift from multiple dates to one only increase it? Wouldn't the women in question attract attention of their own? And then there was the subterfuge and manipulation that such a response would involve. The lying, deception and the complete absence of integrity—everything he strove to avoid.

Given that the three of them were at the top of their game with infinite resources at their disposal, he'd racked his brains for a more mature, less complicated way to protect their reputations. But before he'd been able to come up with anything, Zane's absurd proposal had somehow evolved into a bet, with their Helberg shares as the stake.

'We meet back here on Labor Day,' the man had drawled with a languid smile, as if acquiring the ailing conglomerate was nothing more to him than a game. 'Winner takes all accumulated shares and has an unimpeded run at Helberg. Two birds. One stone.'

While Cade had gone along with the mad idea, Adam had reeled, scarcely been able to believe his ears. This solution to the twin problems of the reputational impact of the article and the stalemate surrounding the company they all wanted had felt farcical. Surreal. Ill thought out at the very least, and he'd protested these points. But ultimately he hadn't been able to see how else they were to keep the share price down and determine who got Helberg. As Zane had coolly pointed out, the likelihood of them stepping out of each other's way just because he—Adam—had asked nicely was zero.

So he'd accepted the bet. He'd had no choice. No matter how important his principles, he was not forfeiting Helberg. He needed it to right the wrong that had been a festering thorn in his side for years. Only when he'd reclaimed Montague's would he find some kind of peace from the torment of knowing that because he'd declined his mother's call the night she'd overdosed he was responsible for her death. Only then would he be free of the guilt that was preventing him from exploring a proper relationship with his sister, Charley. Vengeance and justice would appease his conscience, he was sure. Therefore, he had to play the game and play to win.

After leaving the gym on Saturday morning, he'd checked out the *Blush* article, which had been just as inaccurate yet as salacious as he'd feared, and the 'one-date wonders' hashtag, which had been worse.

Realising he needed to nip any fallout in the bud, he'd immediately called an extraordinary pre-emptive board meeting. He'd spent an hour soothing the ruffled feathers of those who'd caught wind of the story and had then moved on to reassurances that his standing—and that of the company—would remain intact.

That evening, he'd attended the event that had prevented him from insisting to Cade and Zane that the terms of the bet required celibacy and involved no unwitting women in it at all. He couldn't have cried off the company's Fourth of July extravaganza when he was hosting the bloody thing. He hadn't even been able to ditch his date for the event because Annabel St James was the face of the Courtney Collection's leading cosmetics brand, which had just launched a new five-hundred-dollar face cream whose sales would benefit from as much publicity it could get.

Instead, he'd capitalised on the situation by asking her to do him a favour and, for the next couple of months, feed any speculation that they were dating. Annabel—an old friend he'd known since school—had recalled that he'd once done the same for her to deflect some tiresome speculation about her own sexual preferences and agreed.

At least she wouldn't get the wrong idea about the nature of their relationship, he thought darkly as he sat down at his desk and fired up his computer. There was no danger of her wanting more than he could ever give. He was never settling down for real. For that to happen, he imagined he'd have to embrace the chaos of desire and emotion, and even the *thought* of it turned his blood to ice.

Short discreet flings with women who posed no

threat to his control were more than adequate for his needs. He had no wish to pursue the kind who tempted him into recklessness in the compact bathroom of a cocktail bar, who blew his mind and then left him there dazed and confused, and who subsequently stormed into his thoughts and dominated his dreams with alarming and unexpected regularity until he'd forced himself to shove her from his head once and for all. That had been a blip.

He wasn't cut out for love or family anyway. To him, that word didn't conjure up images of loud happy dinners round the table and warm cosy thoughts of unconditional love and support. It meant a father who'd preferred the company of much younger women to that of his wife and children and who'd liked to party hard even into middle age. A mother who'd been so miserable in her marriage that she'd wasted away in the castle in Northumberland before life had become too wretched to bear. A sister who, because he'd been away at school when she'd been born, he'd never really got to know but had let down nevertheless. It meant dysfunction so severe that if they hadn't had billions in the bank, they'd have been on the radar of social services.

So Annabel was perfect for the situation in which he now found himself. He'd secured one woman for the entirety of the summer, and though it pained him to admit it, Zane had been right about the effect of that tactic. The half dozen paparazzi that had gathered outside his Central Park West apartment block had gone by the time he'd left home at the crack of dawn this morning, which meant that he was no longer a one-date wonder. His reputation was safe.

All he had to do now was sit back and wait for Cade and Zane to knock themselves out of the contest, and Helberg Holdings would be his. He didn't imagine it would take long. There was no way on earth either man would be able to limit himself to one woman for the next nine weeks. Not only did they go through the opposite sex as if the human race were on the verge of extinction, but also, they weren't nearly as driven as he was.

Cade seemed more bothered by the article and its effect on his PR team, and Zane clearly considered the whole thing nothing more than a source of entertainment. The text message he'd sent ten minutes ago was evidence of that. It had contained a photo of him—Adam—and Annabel at the party, entwined in a deliberately intimate embrace. Zane had captioned the photo with Could do worse for the summer! and a winking emoji.

Adam had rolled his eyes at the puerility of the message, but it was gratifying to know that his efforts had produced the desired result, and so soon. Now he could look to the fortnight ahead and the annual financial audit, which, this year more than most, needed to go without a hitch because the battle for Helberg wouldn't be completely won on Labor Day. Even after taking possession of Cade's and Zane's shares, he'd still need to hoover up the rest. Unlike Zane, he wasn't in the business of hostile takeovers. He'd have to woo the remaining stakeholders, and they'd be more likely to greenlight the deal if the credentials of the Courtney Collection were as spotless as could be.

Therefore, he would be laying out the red carpet for the people his father had scathingly described as 'bean counters,' the auditors who were due to arrive any moment now. He would see that their every requirement was satisfied. He'd be available for consultation 24-7, on hand to deal with anything that arose personally, which was why he'd had his secretary relocate the team from the basement to his domain up here and cancel any imminent travel arrangements he had.

He could not afford another hit to his reputation or that of the company should something be amiss. Both needed to remain squeaky clean until the acquisition of Helberg was tied up. He would allow nothing to go wrong and jeopardise the absolution he'd been pursuing for months and was now within such close reach. Nothing.

There were more disagreeable places to be spending the next two weeks before going on some much-needed leave, Ella mused as she glanced around in appreciation, then headed for the lift to which she'd been directed. Such as the noisy, cold, out-of-town manufacturing plant, where she'd been scheduled to go right up until seven this morning when she'd received instructions to divert to this team instead.

The twenty-five-storey Courtney Collection tower

had been constructed thirty years ago. Its highly complex postmodern Art Deco design was said to resemble the fall of a skirt over a bent knee. It was clad in glass that was green on the left and white on the right, lit with multicoloured neon at night and had won widespread praise from architectural critics.

Inside, the extravagantly airy lobby oozed controlled, refined elegance. A palate of soft creams and taupe exuded expensive and exquisite sophistication. In between acres of glass that granted a view of Madison Avenue, tastefully abstract art hung on the walls and pale Italian travertine tiles covered the floor. Even the air smelled divine.

She'd read briefly, in the blissfully air-conditioned cab on the way in, that the Courtney Collection was the world's largest luxury goods empire. It had one hundred offices on five continents. Vineyards in France and Australia. Seven-star boutique hotels in London, Paris and Rome. And upmarket retail spaces selling clothes, jewellery, perfumes and cosmetics in every fashionable corner of the globe.

Far more importantly, however, it offered her the chance of a long-awaited, well-deserved promotion.

In the aftermath of her regrettable affair with Drew Taylor, her then boss's then boss, her career had stalled. She had not moved a rung up the ladder, as she'd previously expected. She'd continued as team leader on small, low-profile audits, and she had received neither a pay rise nor a bonus in a year.

A coincidence? When Drew had been transferred

to the other side of the country to head up the office there? She didn't think so. But she'd had no solid evidence of discriminatory treatment, and even if she had, she doubted she'd have done anything with it. The moral high ground could be a lonely place. Word travelled. She'd have likely been eased out of the firm and might never have worked in the industry she loved again, and she'd fought too hard to risk everything.

It had taken an immense amount of courage and determination to finish high school and attend college when, on that front, expectations both at home and in the classroom had been virtually non-existent. She'd had to be incredibly strong to stay out of trouble in an environment that seethed with it and retain the belief that unlike her parents, she didn't have to deal drugs for a living. Once she'd decided at the age of fourteen that acquiring a profession was going to be her way out—accountancy, since she was good with numbers—she'd pursued it with dogged determination. She'd found the library. She'd researched and contacted charities that would help. She'd blagged her way into jobs in town to fund her studies and kept her endeavours quiet. Later on, she'd shed the visible stain of her upbringing by taking elocution and etiquette lessons and learned to network. She'd done whatever it took to graduate top of her class. She'd had her pick of jobs and she hadn't looked back.

Briefly, stupidly, she'd lost sight of her goals, but she would not double down on her mistake. So instead of filing a complaint, instead of risking unemployment by resigning, she'd shoved a lid on her anger and bitterness and kept her head down. She'd bided her time until memories had faded, although her own hadn't because she still couldn't believe she'd been so reckless.

What had she been thinking? was the question that had hammered her for days after the affair had come to light when she'd accidentally messaged her boss instead of her lover. How could she have lowered her guard the night her department had gone out to celebrate the end of a successful financial year? Sure, there'd been gallons of champagne, and after working flat out for months, everyone had been on a high, but that was no excuse for falling into conversation with Drew and flirting. For allowing herself to be flattered by the attentions of an older man. For succumbing to the spark of attraction and then investing far more in it than he had when he'd made her no promises.

Even now she couldn't work out what had been going on in her head. She'd lost focus. She'd let herself down badly. Because of the fallout, she'd ceded control of her career for the first time ever. She was still as furious with herself as she was with HR and Drew over what had happened. But playing the long game—however frustrating and unfair it had felt—finally seemed to be paying off.

Thanks to the previous incumbent coming down with a virus late last night, she was now leading this team of ten for the next two weeks on an audit that was anything but low key. It had been hinted that on the

back of it, if all went well, she'd be awarded the promotion she should have received twelve months ago,
together with a commensurate pay rise and bonus.

And it *would* go well. Because her year out in the
cold was nearly over. Redemption was so imminent
she could almost taste it. Soon she'd be able to let go
of the rage and regret that consumed so much energy.
And she would allow nothing to threaten any of it.

The doors of the lift opened with a soft swoosh.
Ella pulled her shoulders and lifted her chin, then
emerged into a vast space that was more penthouse
apartment than office. It was triple height and had
two adjacent walls made entirely of glass. Her gaze
flickered around for a moment, taking in the laden
bookshelves, the abstract art and more of the cream-
and-taupe décor. The squishy sofas, the abundant
flower arrangements and the conference table upon
which had been placed a carafe of water, a glass and
a platter of pastries.

But the contents of the room and the stunning view
beyond disappeared the minute she clapped eyes on
the man standing at the top of the staircase on the
mezzanine, radiating power and authority as the
master of all he surveyed, the man she'd known for
twenty earth-shattering minutes four weeks ago and
had never *ever* expected to see again.

For a moment, she stood frozen to the spot, staring up at him in utter shock. The world screeched to
a halt. Her heart gave a great crash against her ribs
and then accelerated until it was beating a thunder-

ing *Oh-God-Oh-God-Oh-God* tattoo. She had to be hallucinating. Because this could not be happening. It simply could not.

But as he set off down the stairs and the world started up again, she realised she *wasn't* hallucinating and this *was* happening. By some horrible coincidence, perfect, sexy smouldering Adam, who'd rocked her foundations and stolen her wits in the restroom of a cocktail bar, was evidently her brand-new client.

And, oh dear God, she thought as a hot clammy sweat broke out all over her skin and she began to hyperventilate, the implications of this for her redemption, for her career, for her future, were not good *at all*.

CHAPTER THREE

WHAT FRESH HELL was this?

Adam strode across the floor towards the woman he thought he'd consigned to the past weeks ago, his pulse thundering, his head spinning in an effort to contain the shock reeling through him. How much more chaos could he be expected to handle? First, the issues with Helberg. Then the mad bet that had had him abandoning his principles and faking a girlfriend. And now Ella from the bar—who'd forced him to take more cold showers in a week than he had in his entire life, who'd stolen his control so comprehensively he'd almost worn a hole in the carpet with all the frustrated early morning pacing he'd done—was no longer a forgettable moment of insanity but actually here, in his office, evidently none other than the lead auditor he'd been told was on her way up.

So much for having hauled everything back under his control, he thought grimly, forcing the breath from his lungs before he passed out. What, precisely, was he going to do about this latest development that had trouble written all over it?

Instinct was urging him to hustle her straight back into the lift and have her escorted off the premises because as he approached her, it was becoming appallingly apparent that her effect on him was as immediate and intense as he recalled. A month ago, she'd decimated fourteen years of steely control with one blink of her beautiful brown eyes, and he was in danger of allowing her to do it again now.

Today, in addition to a sleeveless cream silk top, she was wearing a knee-length fitted skirt the colour of raspberries. And despite the horrified disbelief rampaging through his system, all he could think was, what was she wearing beneath it, if anything? In a flash, it occurred to him then that the sofa to his right was large and accommodating. Within moments she could be sprawled across it while he found out. In his imagination, he saw her long golden hair spread out all over the butter-soft leather with his hands once again tangled in it. He heard the desperate sounds she'd make. He even felt her stiletto heels digging into his back.

But he couldn't get rid of her, dammit. Because, while he sent so much business her accountancy firm's way that he had ample leverage to do so, a response like that would cause a delay to the audit. Disruption. In some quarters—say, among the remaining Helberg Holdings shareholders—such ripples in the water might be seen as indicative of potential problems, which was not an outcome he could allow.

So there'd be no hustling her anywhere. No matter

how much in this moment he might regret choosing that bar and that night to alleviate his colossal stress with whisky, she was staying put.

He could handle the attraction, he assured himself as he came to a stop in front of her and banked the response of his body to her intoxicating proximity. It wouldn't be the first time he'd denied his libido. Overwhelmed with guilt, he'd pretty much given up sex altogether in the aftermath of his mother's death and he'd survived. Once this job was underway, he would keep interaction to a minimum and maintain his distance unless strictly necessary. He had no reason to deliberately seek her out and more than enough work to be getting on with. He would focus on the endgame and keep a clear head. It was only for two weeks. It would pass in a flash.

'Adam Courtney, CEO,' he said, pasting a professional smile to his face and holding out his hand. 'Welcome to the Courtney Collection.'

Ella stared down at the hand that Adam was holding out, disbelief and pique spiralling through the shock that was still wreaking havoc on her system.

He hadn't recognised her.

While she'd spent weeks trying not to recall every single second of what they'd done together, he'd clearly forgotten all about it. He hadn't suffered sleepless nights and feverish flushes that attacked whenever they felt like it. Or experienced any pangs of regret that she'd walked out of that bathroom instead of joining him at the bar for the martini he'd proposed. He'd put her straight from his mind and moved on, as if for him that kind of thing wasn't a frenzied moment of madness but an everyday occurrence. Nothing out of the ordinary. Nothing special. And how unflattering *was* that?

But the blow to her pride was something to be analysed at a later date, if at all. Right now, she had to focus on the hammer that was smashing her hopes and dreams to bits and the nausea churning up her stomach as the reality of what was unfolding here hit.

Whether he recognised her or not, their shared history had serious ramifications. That promotion she so badly wanted? Gone. The career she'd worked so damned hard to repair? Back to where it was a year ago. Her future? Very much not mapped out. Because a smooth and successful audit with her in charge was now unthinkable.

How could she possibly stay in the role when there was such a massive and undeniable conflict of interest? Auditing was not a grey area. There were rules and she abided by them, because without integrity, without control, what was there? She wouldn't compromise the standards she'd clung to as she'd battled her way out of poverty and despair, no matter how much she wished right now she could. They were the framework on which she'd built her entire career. She lived, slept and breathed them.

So she couldn't pretend that she hadn't recognised him either, even though that would be so very convenient. She couldn't just sweep this under the carpet and carry on as if her world hadn't imploded. She had to do what was right.

Fighting back the hot fiery ball of frustration, injustice and hopelessness that was barrelling through her, Ella swallowed hard. She lifted her gaze to his, her heart pounding, her throat impossibly tight. 'I need to step aside,' she ground out, having to push every word through her teeth.

Adam dropped his hand and took a step back, his eyes on hers, his smile gone. 'Why?'

'We have a conflict of interest.'

A muscle jumped in his cheek. 'Because we had sex?'

Once again, the floor beneath her feet rocked and her heart practically stopped. A slew of vivid images slammed into her head and a rush of blistering heat propelled a flush to her cheeks.

'So you *do* recognise me,' she said with a breathlessness that appalled her, but at least she was spared the mortification of having to explain *why* there was a problem.

'Of course I do.'

'I thought you'd forgotten who I was.'

His gaze ran over her and she nearly went up in flames. 'On what planet would that be possible?'

'For all I know, you pick up women in bars on a regular basis.'

'I don't. That night was a one-off. And who picked

who up is debatable. I may have made the first move, but you made the last.'

That was true. Wasn't it? She couldn't quite remember. Or think straight. Her restored ego might be cheering with relief, but she'd forgotten how mesmerising his eyes were, how easy it was to fall into them and how good he smelled. Despite the disastrous nature of this situation, tiny flashes of electricity were zinging through her. Heat was pooling between her legs. If she took a step in his direction, she would be within kissing distance. She could lift herself up, wind her arms around his neck and press her mouth to his. She hadn't dared do that the night they'd met. Suspecting she might well weaken and wind up agreeing to the martini and further madness, she'd limited herself to a brush of her lips against his cheek before disappearing. That now felt remiss.

'However, I was intending to forget all about it,' he said, jolting her out of her trance and bringing her back down to earth with a bump.

What? For a second, she just stared at him, her brow furrowing in confusion, the ferocious heat momentarily doused as if a bucket of iced water had been thrown at her. Surely he couldn't have said what she thought he just said.

'You can't mean that,' she said, as baffled as she was astonished.

'Why not?' he replied with cool self-assurance.

'It would be highly unethical.' Why wasn't he concerned? He should have frog-marched her out of this building five minutes ago. She would have if she were him. 'I could get fired. I'd never work again. And the risks would be substantial for you too. The integrity of the audit would be compromised. Your reputation might take a hit.'

That silenced him for a second. Something flared in the depths of his eyes, but it was gone before she could identify it. 'Are you good at your job?'

'Exceptionally.' Which made the situation all the more painful.

'Would what we did have any impact on your work?'

Was he questioning her commitment? Her professionalism? Or was he concerned that, once again unable to control herself in his presence, she might demand he ravish her over the photocopier? 'Absolutely not,' she said, determined to reassure him on all those fronts. 'Nothing gets in the way of that.'

'Do you *want* to stand down?'

The prospect of it cleaved her in two and drove a stake through her chest. 'I can't think of anything I want to do less.'

'Then don't.'

Oh, if only she weren't so principled. If only she'd chosen a different bar in which to drown her sorrows that night. But it was far too late for regrets. 'It's not that simple.'

'Have you told anyone about what we did?'

'No,' she said as a shudder ran through her. Why would she want anyone knowing how weak and im-

pulsive she'd been when she'd told all her friends after
the Drew affair that she was steering clear of men for
the foreseeable future? 'I can barely believe it happened in the first place. It was so out of character.'

'Good. I haven't either.' His jaw lost some of its ri-
gidity, and his expression relaxed a fraction. 'The way
I see it is this. We hardly know each other. We're not
going to have sex again. We don't even need to *refer*
to it again. The conflict of interest is negligible. So
negligible, in fact, that I don't believe there even is
one. So why should you be made to suffer for something that is ultimately irrelevant, when no one knows
about it but us?'

Well, when he put it like that, he made a good case,
she thought, nibbling her lip as she considered the arguments he'd used to bulldoze her objections.

They *didn't* know each other and of *course* they
weren't having sex again. She'd only ever intended it
to be a one-time event. The reason she'd rejected his
offer of a drink that night was because even though
she'd instantly craved another hit of him, she'd sensed
he was lethal. She'd suspected that if she ever found
herself in an actual bed with him, she might never
get out of it, and what impact would *that* have had
on her career? So the disappointment that was surging through her could take a hike. It wasn't happening. Even if he hadn't made it clear he had no further
designs on her, at which she should be feeling relieved and not insulted, she had absolutely no desire
for history to repeat itself by her mixing business

with pleasure again and potentially sacrificing another promotion.

And it *wasn't* fair that twenty minutes of madness a month ago should destroy all the progress she'd made and threaten her future. Especially since, this time, what had happened wasn't even her fault. What they'd done together *was* irrelevant. It *wouldn't* have any effect on her conduct or the outcome of the audit. Her impartiality and objectivity would *never* be at risk.

But what about her principles if she did decide to follow his lead and forget all about what they'd done? How could she treat them with such disrespect when they'd helped her to get where she was? When they'd been her guiding light for over a decade? It didn't bear thinking about. Although, she wouldn't be sacrificing them forever, observed the devil's advocate in her head. She'd merely be temporarily setting them aside for the duration of this one crucial audit, upon which the future of her career depended. She could reclaim them the minute she finished here.

The only fly in the ointment would be the chemistry that unfortunately hadn't diminished one little bit. Her every nerve ending was quivering in response to his proximity. Her temperature was sky high. She'd never considered a white shirt particularly sexy before, but right now she wanted to rip his open and get her hands on his skin.

However, it wasn't as if they'd be having any further contact. This unfortunate meeting was just a courtesy, and once she and her team were set up in the basement or at the end of some dark dingy corridor, liaising directly with the finance department as per usual, she need never lay eyes on him again.

She deserved the opportunity to correct the mistake she'd made a year ago, and ceding control of her career to external forces again wasn't the way to do that. Besides, if she didn't stick with it, there'd be repercussions. She'd have to explain her decision to her colleagues. Her boss. She'd have to confess that, once again, she'd messed up again because of a man. She'd lose the respect she'd been fighting so hard to restore, and this time her career wouldn't just be damaged, it would be over, because she wouldn't be given another chance. She'd be out in the cold for good, and after everything she'd worked for, she simply could not contemplate it. No, she had to see this job through to the end. And she *would* see this job through to the end.

'All right then,' she said, ruthlessly crushing the protest of her principles and channelling cool, clearheaded professionalism instead. 'Just tell me where to go and we'll get started.'

Having neutralised the risk of Ella stepping down and screwing up his plans for a trouble-free audit, Adam relaxed marginally and stalked over to the conference table that was to be her workspace for the next couple of weeks.

Thank God she'd seen the situation his way. Not that there was any other way he could have allowed her to see it. If she'd stuck to her guns and recused herself, she would have made life extremely tricky for the both of them. Then what would he have done? Bribed her? Resorted to threats?

Such underhanded tactics weren't his style, but this set of circumstances was unprecedented. There was no end to which he wouldn't go to get what he wanted, and if that meant taking advantage of the battle between integrity and a burning desire to see the audit through that had played out on her face, then so be it. Whatever the reason, it was clear she wanted this job with a determination that seemed to go beyond mere duty. Something else appeared to be at stake for her here, and he was not above weaponizing her desperation if necessary.

A part of him loathed that he had been forced to put any amount of trust in her when she was such an unknown quantity. The women he generally slept with he chose because they were safe. The attraction they shared caused him no trouble. When he was done, they were gone and he didn't look back. But he hadn't selected Ella. She'd selected him. If she decided to go to the press with details of what they'd got up to, she could obliterate four years of reputational reconstruction in a heartbeat. He'd instantly lose the respect and trust he'd worked so hard to earn. His authority would crumble to dust. He'd be labelled as his father's son.

When Adam had taken over as CEO—following the fatal aneurysm his father had suffered while in bed with a nubile blonde—he'd faced an uphill battle to remove the stain on the family name. There'd been many who'd feared business as usual. One or two who'd benefitted from the gravy train and had expected it to continue.

But he'd been determined to restore the plummeting fortunes of the company that had been in his family for over a century. So he'd fired those members of the board who'd repeatedly vetoed his father's dismissal and put a stop to the bottomless expense account. He'd implemented policies that encouraged reporting bad behaviour and transparency. He'd negotiated loans and trebled the marketing and PR budget.

With the rot gone, the climate—not just at this office but worldwide—had done a full one-eighty within six months. A year later, sales had risen by forty percent and the share price had doubled. Now, the Courtney name on a personal level was associated not with sleaze and corruption but integrity and trust.

Ella had the power destroy all the progress he'd made. She could blow his plans for Helberg Holdings right out of the water, because he well knew that shareholders could be funny about things like sex scandals. However, the conviction in her voice when she'd answered his question about whether she'd told anyone about that night in the bar, as well as her very visible shudder, had not been feigned, and that concern had been allayed. At least, for now.

Had his curiosity been piqued, he might have wondered why discretion seemed to matter as much to her as it did to him and why she was so determined to see the job through. Why she'd put aside her own integrity to do that.

But he wasn't remotely interested in the things they shared or what drove her. He wasn't intrigued by her at all. He certainly wasn't dwelling on the way she'd bitten her lip as she'd considered his arguments and imagining how incendiary kissing her would be. Or regretting that they wouldn't be having sex again. One monumentally reckless loss of control was enough to last a lifetime. Therefore, he would not be indulging the rogue urge to rile her up and get under her skin. Whether she was still as attracted to him as he was to her was utterly irrelevant. They had a job to do and that was all.

So why was she still standing where he'd left her instead of following him to the table she'd be working at for the next two weeks and getting started? Why was she still looking at him as if she couldn't figure out what was going on? Just in case it wasn't blindingly obvious, Adam pulled out a chair and gave it a pat. 'You're over here.'

CHAPTER FOUR

IT TOOK ELLA a good ten seconds to compute the implication of Adam's announcement, by which time he'd waved at her to come on over and poured her a glass of water.

What on earth was the meaning of this? she wondered in alarm, her gaze flicking between the table with the pastries and the man now heading for the stairs that rose to his office on the mezzanine. Why wasn't he directing her to the basement as she'd expected? To the finance department, perhaps? Or even to his secretary for further instructions?

Surely, he didn't intend the audit take place up here on his floor, did he? He had to be out of his mind. She could not work up here with him a matter of metres away. Her concentration would be wrecked. She'd never get anything done.

'Wait,' she said, needing to clarify the situation and fix it immediately if necessary.

Adam stopped in his tracks and whipped round. 'Is there a problem?'

'There could be.'

His brows drew together in a deep frown and she thought she caught a sigh of exasperation. 'What is it now?'

'Am I to understand you wish the audit to take place up here?'

'That is correct.'

She gave her head a sharp shake. 'It's out of the question.'

For a moment, there was utter silence. All Ella could hear was the pounding of her heart in her ears. Then his eyebrows shot up as if he wasn't used to being challenged, and he said, very coolly, 'I beg your pardon?'

His expression was darkening forbiddingly, she noticed, but she refused to be intimidated because he wasn't in charge here. She was. This was *her* audit— a vitally important one—and it was more crucial than usual that common protocol was followed. His ridiculous presumption needed to be corrected, so she lifted her chin, pulled her shoulders back.

'My audit will *not* be taking place up here,' she said, fixing him with a look that had once been called chilling. 'Firstly, from a practical point of view, there wouldn't be nearly enough space for eleven people and everything we require.'

'Which is why you will be up here with me and your team will be occupying the offices one floor down.'

Well, *that* was never going to happen. She and her team needed full and direct access to each other.

She couldn't keep dashing up and down the stairs whenever face-to-face communication was required. It would be massively inconvenient and a complete waste of everyone's time. And then there was the stress of being completely alone with him, the possible intensifying of the attraction and the battle she'd have to fight it. Even hypothetically the thought of it made her feel quite weak.

'Secondly,' she continued, even more determined to prevail, 'a set-up such as the one you suggest could lead to accusations of undue influence. I mean, pastries? The best view in the city? When we're normally stashed away in a musty room at the end of a corridor with windows that look out onto a wall? Our impartiality would be compromised. Questions would be asked. I simply can't allow it.'

But if she'd expected Adam to take on board her undeniably valid point and surrender to her superior experience, she was to be disappointed.

'No questions will be asked,' he countered, folding his arms across his impossibly broad chest as his cool blue gaze bore into hers. 'No one would dare. Proximity is required because I will be overseeing this audit personally. I want to make sure that any problems are knocked on the head the second they arise. Every query you or your team have and every piece of information you require will go through me, so you and I will be liaising directly.'

Ella's stomach clenched. What? No. Absolutely not. 'That would be highly irregular,' she said, refusing to be distracted by the play of muscles she could see going on beneath the crisp white cotton of his shirt and instead mentally running through the consequences of such a strategy, the regulations surrounding neutrality and the headache of having to deal specifically with him.

'In what way?'

'Regardless of the questionable ethics of going through you for everything, your intended degree of involvement would not only add another layer of complication to an already complex investigation, but it would also make the process way more inefficient.'

'I disagree.'

That was his prerogative, but his opinion was irrelevant. 'You're not the expert here.'

'Do finance departments jump to attention the minute you tell them to?'

'Well, no, not always, but—'

'They will if it's me doing the telling,' he said bluntly. 'As will everyone else. They won't be able to work fast enough. I've cleared my diary for the next two weeks. I will be available to you and anyone else who needs me twenty-four-seven.'

In response to that, Ella's head began to throb. Once again, he was trampling over her every objection, only this time his counterarguments didn't make any sort of sense. 'Why?'

Up shot his eyebrows again. 'What do you mean, why?'

'Most CEOs don't take such a personal interest in something as prosaic as the annual financial audit.'

'I'm not most CEOs.'

That was certainly true. He was by far the sexiest CEO she'd ever come across. Tall, lean, powerful... And his forearms—long curves of hard muscle dusted with a smattering of dark masculine hair—really were something else. What would it feel like to be enveloped by all that strength? To have his strong hands on her body, his clever fingers coaxing her to the dizzy heights of pleasure? To be wrapped up once again in heat and passion and excitement?

'I don't see you as the enemy,' he said, bringing her back to the conversation with a bump. 'I believe in working together. Which we can, and will, do.' He tilted his head and regarded her coolly. 'You seem to be under the impression that you can influence what's going on here Ella. But you can't. This is my company and my audit. *I* make the rules, not you. So, if you have a problem with that, I'll just have to find someone to run it who doesn't.'

As his words hit their mark, Ella's blood chilled and her stomach fluttered. The heat whipping through her system fled. The heady desire vaporised. Adam looked calm enough, but there was a trace of steel behind his words. A glint of ruthlessness in his eyes. The ripple of tension in the air told her that he would stop at nothing to get what he wanted and that if she knew what was good for her, she'd surrender.

Suddenly simmering with outrage, she burned with the urge to march up to him and inform him that not only did he *not* make the rules that he was breaking left right and centre, despite his apparent wish to avoid trouble, but also that threatening the auditors was not a good move.

But she couldn't, dammit. Because, for one thing, when she got too close to him, her brain malfunctioned. And for another, whatever the reason for his stubborn insistence on the status quo, whether he saw this as some kind of a game or was simply a control freak, the truth was he held all the cards. She couldn't afford to antagonise him. If he acted on this power trip of his and got her thrown off the job, she could wind up unemployed, her career in ruins. She'd instantly lose everything. The condo she'd just bought would be repossessed. The security and empowerment that earning her own money gave her would disappear overnight. What would she do then? Where would she go? How would she survive?

She wasn't going to throw away everything she'd worked so hard for and jeopardise the future she deserved over a tussle for control. The late nights of study, the exhaustion, the doubts that she was good enough to make it weren't going to be for nothing. Like him, she would do whatever it took to get what she wanted, and right now it was clear that that meant keeping him onside until the audit was done and the financial records signed off.

So no matter how much she hated that he kept forcing her to make decisions that challenged her integrity, no matter how churned up he made her feel inside, she had no choice but to acquiesce. Somehow she would maintain the audit's independence. She would

never let him see how bothered she was by the idea
of the two of them working up here together alone.
She could certainly contain the attraction she still felt
for him. She had far too much at stake to let that get
the better of her.

'Fine,' she said, with a cool smile and a deliberately
casual shrug, as if she weren't bothered by the outcome of the conversation—or him—at all. 'You win.'

Once she'd wrestled her frustration at being thwarted
under some sort of control and checked the regulations concerning impartiality, Ella headed downstairs
to greet the team and make sure that everyone knew
what they were doing—which they did because, unlike
her, they'd had weeks to prepare. Then she returned
to the penthouse, set herself up and turned her attention to work, determined to put her infuriating client
firmly from her head.

Unfortunately, however, this turned out to be easier said than done.

By virtue of the fact that she'd been parachuted into
this assignment at the last minute, she was going to
have to work doubly hard and longer hours to keep on
top of things. So she could not afford to waste even a
second, let alone great chunks of time.

Yet that was precisely what happened. More calls
than she cared to count went to voicemail. Files that
should have been opened instantly weren't. And all
because, whether he was at his desk or wandering

around his office on the phone, the man up there on the mezzanine was just too darn distracting.

To her despair, the ruthlessness she'd witnessed earlier hadn't diminished his appeal in the slightest. On the contrary, every time she thought about it, shameful thrills of excitement shot through her.

In spite of her best efforts to stop it, her gaze slid in his direction with frustrating predictability. Her imagination, which had never troubled her before she'd met him, had gone into overdrive. She kept envisaging heading up the stairs and sidling into his office, where he'd invite her to come on over and make herself comfortable on his lap. Or perhaps he'd make his way down to her, clear the table with one sweep of his arm and lift her onto it. Either way, they ended up in a wholly unacceptable clinch.

This disruption to her concentration did not bode well for a trouble-free audit to be completed within the specified time frame, so after lunch Ella attempted to do something about it.

First, she shifted her position so that he wasn't in her direct vision, in the hope that out of sight would be out of mind. But that didn't work because, apparently, her awareness of him was all-encompassing. Then she tried loitering downstairs with her team, but the unproductivity of such a move was just too annoying to pursue.

She hated that controlling her response to him was proving such a challenge. She hated even more that he didn't appear to be remotely bothered by her, which was insane, because the last thing she needed was the added stress of the attraction turning out to be mutual.

But she would not allow another man she'd slept with to mess with her head and jeopardise her career, so she eventually figured she'd just have to double down on her efforts. If she was to stand any chance of not screwing this job up, she had to get a grip and focus. She had to keep what was at stake for her at the forefront of her mind and start acting like the professional she was.

So she stuck Post-it notes adorned with the word *PROMOTION!!!* to various items that surrounded her. She allowed herself to imagine in full dreadful detail how her life might fall apart should this audit go wrong—the humiliation, the uncertainty, the peril. Every time her gaze threatened to drift in his direction, she forced herself to recall her last performance review, during which she'd been told that she wasn't quite ready for the next step up, and that snapped it straight back to the laptop.

Although it took considerable effort, to her relief, these strategies worked. Largely managing to ignore Adam's existence, she soon found confidence in her spreadsheets and settled into the role. Being on a different floor to her team turned out not to be as problematic as she'd expected, and over the next couple of days they made excellent progress, aided, she had to admit, by the degree of his involvement, which—both annoyingly and pleasingly—*had* resulted in improved efficiency and ultra-quick results.

Ella wasn't prone to pettiness, but she couldn't deny that she'd relished bombarding him with emails, some of which didn't actually require his attention. She wanted to make him pay for effectively holding her ransom by spamming his inbox. She wanted him to sorely regret forcing her to bend to his will. However, she was thwarted in those endeavours too, because not once did he tell her to desist. No matter how trivial or important the request, each was handled promptly without either comment or complaint.

There were only two issues to which she was having trouble getting a response. One was an unaccounted-for trip to London in the company's private jet back in August last year. The other was the steady yet rapid purchase of millions of shares in a multinational called Helberg Holdings, whose portfolio was so sprawling yet in such trouble that no one could work out what he was doing with it.

Both anomalies had raised a flag with her team. Neither had yet been addressed, despite her repeated efforts to do so. Frustratingly, Adam had ignored the half dozen reminders she'd sent him, so on Wednesday afternoon she decided to tackle him directly.

Setting her jaw, practically vibrating with resolve, she picked up a notepad and pen and headed up the stairs to his office. 'Do you have a moment to go through some queries?' she said, trying not to notice how the sun streaming in through the acres of glass was giving him a corona that made him look like some sort of a god.

'Not right now, I'm afraid,' he replied as he pushed his chair back and got to his feet. 'I'm about to head off for a meeting.'

'When will you be back?'

'I'm not sure. It could go on for a while.'

'I thought you said you'd cleared your diary for the next two weeks.'

'This one's unavoidable.'

With a tight smile, he strode past her and out through the door before she could protest any further. And to her extreme irritation the meeting of his went on for so long that she didn't see him for the rest of the day.

Undeterred, however, she tried again the following morning. But on that occasion she didn't even manage to say a single word to him, because the minute she appeared at his door, he picked up his phone and said coolly, 'Do excuse me, I need to take this,' and that was that for the next two hours.

By Thursday evening, he'd left her with no choice but to take more drastic action. Determined to pin him down, she saw her opportunity when he left his office and headed for the lift. She slipped through the doors just before they closed, trapping them together, a move she regretted almost immediately when her lungs tightened and her head spun, as if all the oxygen had been sucked out of the space. How could she have forgotten what happened when she got too close to him? she wondered for one dizzying moment. Clearly, concentrating on work and being ignored by him these last few days had lulled her into a false sense of security.

But she would not be derailed from the plan, no matter what his effect on her, so halfway into the lift's descent she hit the alarm, causing it to judder to an abrupt halt.

'Why did you do that?'

Adam's vaguely amused tone belied the stony glare he gave her. She ignored the rash of goose bumps breaking out all over her skin, the flare of heat and the quivering of her nerve endings, and focused. 'We need to talk.'

'And what exactly do you need to say that couldn't have been said in my office?'

'That's the trouble. Nothing of significance *was* being said in your office. All I heard were excuses.'

He didn't even respond to that. He just let his glittering gaze drift over her before it settled on her mouth and lingered.

'You know what happens when you and I find ourselves trapped together in confined spaces,' he said, his voice seeming to drop an octave while her lips tingled and her mouth dried. 'I realise we weren't going to refer to that night again, but what else am I to read into this manoeuvre of yours other than invitation?'

In response to that, Ella's heart gave a great lurch and then began to race. He was right. What was she doing? Instead of focusing on getting the answers she wanted, her head was clearing of everything but the urge to push him up against the polished walnut wall and kiss him the way she imagined in the early hours of the morning when she couldn't sleep. What would he do if she did? Fire her? Or would he bury one hand in her hair and lift her skirt with the other, then tackle his belt, his zip, his underwear, and within seconds be thrusting deep inside her, driving her to the dazzling heights of pleasure she'd only experienced with him?

The former seemed more likely, she thought, her head spinning like a top. He was so cool. So contained. He'd shown no sign of being troubled by their continuing attraction. So what did he mean by bringing up that night? Why the seductive tones? Was he messing with her, playing mind games to remind her who was in command?

Well, right now, that evidently wasn't her. In hindsight, this plan had been a terrible idea. So before her last few functioning brain cells disintegrated and she acted on the wild desire suddenly crashing through her, she pulled herself together and jabbed the button to restart the lift.

'You're right,' she said, consoling herself with the knowledge that she could try again tomorrow. With space. With air. Somehow. 'My mistake.'

And when they reached the ground floor—in a matter of seconds, although it felt like an hour—she didn't flee into the night as if the hounds of hell were snapping at her heels. Instead, she lifted her chin, gave him a cool smile and bade him a pleasant goodnight.

CHAPTER FIVE

INITIALLY, ELLA'S SUBMISSION to his will on Monday morning had given Adam one hell of a buzz. Yes, se-curing her compliance had been vital for a number of business-related reasons, so on that level it had been a much-needed win. But there'd been something else mixed up in it too. Regaining the sense of control that had rapidly started diminishing in her dangerously distracting presence had felt critical, and seeing her forced to accept his command, to play by *his* rules, had been not only deeply satisfying but also unex-pectedly exhilarating.

However, the buzz had not lasted long. Nor had the plan he'd come up with the instant he'd realised that the past had collided with the present and his lead au-ditor was a woman with whom he'd shared one explo-sive encounter and to whom he was, inconveniently, still very much attracted.

Determined the audit would proceed without any further upset, he'd succeeded in staying out of her way as much as possible, in confining himself to his office and communicating entirely through email.

But as for keeping his eyes off her, well, in that he'd failed dismally. When she was on the phone, the throaty timbre of her voice wound through him, a ribbon of fire heating every inch of his body. Every time she sashayed across the carpet to the lift, to the coffee machine, to the photocopier, he found himself tracking the sway of her hips. At one point she'd stretched, lifting her arms above her head and arching her back as she eased out the kinks in her neck, and it had taken every drop of self-control that he possessed to contain his body's response to the sight of her breasts straining against the silky fabric of her top.

Even Maggie, his secretary, had noticed his discomfort. 'Is there something wrong with the way the audit's going?' she asked him when she popped up to run through his diary for August.

'No,' he muttered. 'Why?'

'You're staring at Miss Green as if you're trying to vaporise her with the power of your stare.'

Cursing the fact that it was turning out to be far more difficult than he'd expected to keep a grip on the disturbingly intense attraction, he instantly snapped his attention from the woman who was wreaking havoc on his equilibrium to the one who did her utmost to maintain it, and vowed to double down on his efforts to focus by immersing himself in the deluge of emails Ella had started sending him.

The first had dropped into his inbox on Tuesday morning, and thereafter he'd received one virtually every fifteen minutes. Frequently, they contained a single point. He could see no reason why, say, six could not be amalgamated into one, which meant she was doing it deliberately.

But if her aim had been to annoy him, she'd failed. In fact, he found her passive-aggressive attempt at control really rather amusing, and that was another reason he took great care to respond to each and every one with equal gravity.

With two notable exceptions.

Both of which were causing him grief.

First was the flight to London last August that apparently lacked the paperwork to match the log book.

The minute he'd heard that his sister, Charley, was buying a flat with the last of her savings from her ill-fated career as a model, he'd instantly felt compelled to check it out. He hadn't thought twice about dropping everything and commandeering the company plane to get him to her before she signed the contract. His sole concern had been that she was only twenty-one and had a tendency to be reckless—especially with money. She'd had a chequered adolescence, quitting school and getting spotted by an agency, and although she'd managed to pull herself back on track after leaving that world behind, he couldn't be certain she didn't still make impulsive decisions.

He'd had nothing except her best interests at heart, but to his astonishment, she had not been pleased when he'd turned up unannounced at the perfectly acceptable two-bedroom flat in an up-and-coming area of East London. In response to his offer of advice, she'd had a go at him about his need to control everything and everyone. She'd railed at his inability to trust her, insisting that she wasn't a kid any more, that she'd learned from her mistakes, and when the hell was he going to realise that? Would he *ever* let her forget the time he'd had to bail her out of a cell in Barcelona for swearing at a police officer? Or the occasion she'd run away from school and had wanted him to send her the train fare to get to London? When would he start taking her seriously and treat her like the savvy businesswoman she was?

He'd been more affected by the confrontation than he cared to admit. It had taken him weeks to get over the sharp sting of rejection. Even longer to accept that she'd made some very valid points.

Not that he considered his deep-seated need for control a problem. It was essential to contain the chaos he knew he was capable of. Without it, he feared being overrun with the personality traits he'd inherited from his father, with recklessness, and then everything he'd worked for going up in smoke.

As CEOs they were polar opposites. Adam hadn't generated tabloid headlines that crashed the company's share price. He'd never appeared in blurry photos indicating rampant drug use. And he'd certainly never indulged in the sort of inappropriate behaviour at the office that ended up in a lawsuit.

But in other respects, they were worryingly similar. He was the spitting image of his old man, a constant reminder every time he looked in the mirror of who he would turn into if he didn't keep himself in check. As an adolescent screwing around without a thought for anyone other than himself, he'd behaved like him too, and because of that selfishness, his mother had died. On the ultra-rare occasion his willpower failed these days—such as five weeks ago in a cocktail bar bathroom—his true nature roared to the surface with no consideration of the consequences.

And as for controlling his environment and the people around him, well, he was responsible for the livelihoods of quarter of a million employees and revenue that ran into the tens of billions. How else was he to manage that?

But while he had no intention of apologising for his need to keep a tight grip on things, he did want to work on trusting Charley. He wanted to get to know her without the guilt he felt at robbing her of their mother getting in the way. Relationships of the romantic kind were out of the question. Indulging the sort of desire that led to impulsivity and left destruction in its wake turned his stomach. Envisaging the chaos caused by emotion made his head ache. And the thought of being responsible for someone else's happiness and well-being when he was so ill-equipped to care for such things brought him out in a cold sweat. But he hoped to attempt a familial one with his sister.

None of this was up for discussion, however. With Ella or anyone else. Nor was Helberg Holdings, the second item that she was so keen to quiz him about. Even if he had wanted to share details of why the company was

so important to him—Montague's in particular—he
wouldn't know where to start. With his father's philandering? With his mother's abject misery in her marriage
and the one affair her unhappiness had driven her to?
Would he tell her how, in retaliation, a hypocritical,
vengeful Edward Courtney had sold the international
jewellery business she'd worked for and loved so much
to Helberg for a dollar? Would he then move on to his
own role in his mother's suicide and confess to the guilt
he still carried?

No.

All of that would remain strictly private. Only he
knew the full story. Even Charley, who'd been just a
kid when it had happened, was only aware of some
of it.

He didn't particularly enjoy skulking around and
disappearing whenever Ella hove into view, her jaw
set with resolve. It smacked of cowardice and went
against his confronting-problems-head-on approach.
This evening's encounter in the lift had been particularly challenging. Her move had taken him by surprise. Once he'd got over his shock, with awareness
suddenly ripping through him like wildfire, he'd been
gripped by a ferocious surge of the rashness he fought
so hard to contain. He'd wanted to back her up against
the wall and kiss her until she couldn't think straight.
To then strip her naked and sink into her, despite the
security camera embedded in the ceiling.

How he'd stayed calm enough to de-escalate the
situation, he had no idea. It was clear now that the

only reason he'd been able to keep the desire he had for her under control was by maintaining his distance.

It was equally obvious that she was turning out to be unexpectedly tenacious, and he did not want her prodding around his psyche, because who knew what she might then get him to disclose in a moment of weakness? He couldn't stall her for much longer, however. At some point he would have to figure out how to give her the bare minimum of detail and shut these lines of enquiry down.

But for now, he had a stay of execution. Because he'd just received a call from the office in Madrid with news of potential strike action at a clothing factory outside Valencia, so he was on his way to Spain.

And when he returned, that would not be the only problem he'd have fixed. He'd also have shored up his defences so solidly that, come Monday, he'd be able to stand within a metre of Ella Green and not lose his head.

On Friday morning Ella arrived at the office unsure how to proceed, slightly nervous about seeing Adam again, and wondering how on earth she was going to keep the attraction under control after nearly assaulting him in the lift. Unfortunately, overnight, she'd been plagued by dreams about what had happened, but in them she hadn't backed down. She'd told him to take her up on her invitation instead and had woken up at four hot and shivery and unable to get back to sleep, which did not help her composure one little bit.

But it seemed she had nothing to worry about because Adam didn't show up to the office. She had no idea where he was. He replied to her email enquiring into his whereabouts with a vague, unsatisfying *Something's come up.* After that, radio silence. Even his secretary was cryptically obscure when she probed.

At first, she appreciated the chance to restore her self-possession in his absence. However, by 7:00 p.m. she'd come to the conclusion that none of what had happened in the past few days was a coincidence. In fact, she thought darkly as she pushed through the revolving door and out into the warm evening air, it felt like avoidance. For some reason Adam was stonewalling her, deflecting her—deliberately, she suspected when she thought of the extraordinary encounter in the lift—and now he was nowhere to be found.

It was pissing her off. Not because she was remotely interested in what exactly was problematic about these particular queries, or what he had to hide. She wasn't. All that mattered to her was that he was holding things up. He was jeopardising the time frame of the audit and it could not be allowed continue. The schedule was tight as it was, given the size and complexity of the job. It must not overrun. Her promotion depended on finishing on time. The leave she'd booked for the three weeks after—the first she'd taken in over a year—depended on finishing within the allotted fortnight. She was not having both her short-term and long-term future disrupted by him. She wasn't having anything disrupted at all.

So, having somehow managed to subtly wheedle out of Maggie, his secretary, that Adam would be at home tonight, Ella had come up with a plan. Not an entirely ethical one, admittedly, but he'd left her with no choice. Desperate means called for desperate measures. Enough was enough. He would avoid her no more. He would not wrong-foot her again. Or succeed with threats, because she was far too embedded in the process to be ousted from it now. She would get the answers she needed, and she would get them tonight.

Adam had spent all day containing the threat of strike action at his Valencia factory and ensuring there'd be no further trouble. Having accomplished that by late afternoon, and secure in the knowledge that the staff had been appeased—before anyone had gone to the press, thank God—he'd travelled back to New York satisfied that the impact on the company's reputation and the Helberg acquisition in particular was negligible.

Dropping his keys on the table in the hall and abandoning his suitcase, he strode into the white, minimalist living space, then headed for the bar. As a result of criss-crossing the Atlantic twice in less than twenty-four hours, he didn't know what time it was. He couldn't remember when he'd last slept. He was exhausted and stressed beyond belief. He couldn't shake a strange sense of foreboding, the feeling that everything he was trying to achieve balanced on a knife edge, and all he wanted to do was crack open a bottle of whisky and crash out for the next two days.

However, he'd barely had time to down half a glass of single malt when there was a knock at his door. Too spaced out to wonder who it could be when he'd had no warning of a visitor, he set his glass on the bar and went to investigate. Calling down to the concierge didn't occur to him. Neither did looking through the spyhole. So when he opened the door and came face to face with Ella, he was totally unprepared.

Reeling with shock, he wondered for a moment whether he could be hallucinating, the whisky stronger than he'd assumed, perhaps. But unfortunately, she was all too real. He could tell by the way the hairs at the back of his neck were standing on end and her scent, which was winding through him and scrambling his head.

'What the hell are you doing here?' he practically growled, thinking, *God, this week.* How much more could he be expected to endure?

'I could ask you the same thing,' she said, chin up, jaw set. 'Why aren't you at the office? Where have you been?'

'Spain.'

Her eyebrows shot up. 'Spain?'

'A business matter that required my attention. Strike action at one of my factories. How did you find out where I live?'

'Your address was at the top of an invoice,' she said without a trace of shame. 'I told the concierge I was bringing you a birthday surprise and he let me in. I must admit, I was expecting getting access to you to be a lot harder. Your security is terrible.'

Adam fought the urge to grind his teeth. 'This is a gross invasion of privacy.'

'You only have yourself to blame. You've been avoiding me all week.'

'A company the size of mine doesn't run itself.'

'What happened to being available twenty-four-seven?'

Right, he thought, thrown off balance for a moment. He had promised that. But he couldn't do this now. He was shattered and feeling more than a little unhinged. Combined with all that, her proximity was wreaking havoc on him. His hands itched to touch her. It was taking every drop of control he possessed not to move towards her. He had the unnerving feeling that he'd missed the edginess she drummed up in him these last twenty-four hours.

'You need to leave,' he said, a bead of sweat running down his spine, his pulse thudding heavily as he tightened his grip on the door-frame to his left and the door-knob to his right.

'Not until you tell me about the trip to London and Helberg Holdings.'

'I fail to see their relevance.'

'*I'll* assess their relevance.'

'You can wait until Monday.'

'No. I can't.'

'Why not?'

'Because the time frame is slipping, and I won't allow further delay.' She planted her hands on her hips, her eyes shimmering with determination and challenge. 'This audit *has* to finish on Friday, not least because I go on three weeks' leave immediately afterwards. You're holding things up. Deliberately, I suspect. And I don't get it. One minute you're striding about the place dictating how things are going to go and insisting that you be involved in every step of the process—although why you're taking such a close personal interest in things, I still have absolutely no idea—the next you're nowhere to be seen. What's going on?'

'Nothing's going on.'

'London, Adam,' she said, with the strength of will that in any other situation he'd admire, the strength of will that suggested that she wasn't going away and he couldn't just close the door on her because she'd simply bang on it until he opened it again.

He had to give her something, if only to get her to shut up and go away. He'd keep it brief. 'I went to see my sister.'

'Is she employed by the company?'

'No.'

'What does she do?'

'She has her own dress design business called Trouble Maker.'

'Is it, or was the trip in any way related to the Courtney Collection?'

'No.'

'The jet is a company asset. You should not be making personal use of it.'

'Crunch the numbers and tell me what I owe.'

The look she gave him suggested she didn't think much of that idea. 'And what about Helberg Holdings?'

No, that was too much. Explaining London was one thing, but he couldn't go into Helberg now. He didn't think he'd be able to stand having to deal with the memories that dredged up on top of everything else. Not with his composure so badly frayed. 'Quit while you're ahead, Ella.'

'I have no intention of quitting anything.'

He stifled a growl of frustration. 'You're driving me insane.'

'All I'm trying to do is my job, and I'm not going to apologise for being tenacious. I've had to work exceptionally hard to get where I am. I've faced obstacles virtually every step of the way. A decrepit trailer for a home in a park rife with danger. Dead-beat parents. Lousy high school. At one point I was working three jobs to earn the money I needed to study. Only once have I screwed up so badly my career nearly went down the drain. But I won't do it again. And I won't let you mess this up for me. So you *will* answer my questions. This audit *will* finish on Friday and I *will* get that promotion, even if it kills me.'

For a moment, Adam's head spun. The information she'd just hurled at him was too much to process. Obstacles? A trailer? When had she screwed up? What promotion was she talking about? 'That's not what I meant.'

'Then what did you mean?' she demanded, her cheeks flushed, the pulse at the base of her neck fluttering wildly.

'You've been causing me trouble since the minute you showed up on Monday,' he said, thinking that if scaring her off had worked in the lift yesterday, it would work again today. 'You're in my head all the damn time. You threaten my control and make me want to cross lines that I have sworn not to cross. I still want you badly, Ella, and I'm used to taking what I want. There's only so much pressure I can withstand, and my patience is about to snap. You have no idea how close you came to being ravished in the lift last night. Right now, I am seconds away from losing it completely and kissing you until neither of us can think straight. So if you have any sense at all, you'll go home this minute. Because if you don't, if you stay for even a second longer, I will pull you into my apartment and you will not leave until Monday morning. So *my* question to *you*, Ella, is do you want that? Do you want to spend the weekend in my bed?'

He stopped, his head nothing more than rushing white noise, his blood roaring in his ears. The silence thundered. Ella just stared at him, evidently rendered speechless by his words. Her eyes were wide and dark. Her breathing was shallow and ragged. The seconds ticked by like hours. Then, just when he thought she finally understood the danger she was in, she breathed a shuddery, 'God, *yes*,' and launched herself at him.

There was no time for shock. No time to wonder whether she had completely lost her mind. Or whether he had. The minute she was pressed up against him—her arms around his neck, her hands in his hair, her mouth on his like fire—pure instinct took over. He drew her into a crushing embrace, one hand clamped to the back of her head, the other on the small of her back. She moaned, immediately melting into him so that all he could feel was softness and warmth, and he took command, angling her head and deepening the kiss.

She tasted of heaven and he couldn't get enough. His exhaustion was history. Adrenaline was surging through him, zapping his nerve endings until they were on fire. He was on the point of doing as he'd promised, pulling her into his apartment and kicking the door shut when just as suddenly as the kiss had started, it stopped. Ella froze in his arms and jerked back. Her gorgeous brown eyes were glazed. Her hair was mussed and her cheeks flushed.

But right in front of him, the dazed passion on her face turned to distress. She clapped a hand to her mouth and shook her head, her eyes filling with horror and regret. And while he fought for breath, grappled to contain the rampaging need he had for her, tried and failed to make sense of what was going on, she wrenched herself out of his arms, spun on her heel and fled.

CHAPTER SIX

ELLA BURST OUT of Adam's building into the warm evening air, her breathing choppy, her heart banging frantically in her chest, while the only thought whipping round her head was, what had she done? What had she *done*?

How could she have lost control like that? What had she been thinking? She'd turned up at his door all professional guns blazing, on a mission from which she'd sworn she would not deviate. She'd ignored the flicker of concern she'd felt at how tired and drawn he'd looked. She'd noted that he hadn't seemed quite as in control of himself as usual but had immediately quashed the curiosity. With superhuman effort, she'd even managed to contain the surge of desire that had nearly taken out her knees. She'd kept to the plan and stuck determinedly to the script—until he'd told her that she drove him insane and all hell had let loose.

It was one thing giving him a potted version of her background to justify the persistence that annoyed him so much, she thought, hailing a cab with a hand that was still trembling, her head still whirling as if she were on a Waltzer. But she should never have told him that she'd once made a mistake that had messed up her career. She should never have revealed that she was dependent on this audit for a promotion when she'd already provided her upcoming leave as a perfectly valid reason for her desire to get things wrapped up on time. And she should never *ever* have kissed him.

Yet, once again, his nearness had destroyed her brain. With all that dark powerful energy swirling around them, all she'd been able to think with the one brain cell that hadn't been paralysed with shock was that despite his outward composure, he wanted her. As much as she wanted him. Her struggles with the electrifying attraction were also his. Contrary to what she'd thought, he wasn't unaffected by her at all.

That mind-blowing realisation, along with the heat that had burned in his gaze, had crushed what few defences she had against him to dust. The wave of need that had thundered through her had driven out all rational thought. She'd never craved a kiss so much. For days, she'd secretly wondered how it would be. Well, now she knew. He felt like strength and security and he tasted like fire and whisky.

But she'd crossed a line. For all the promises she'd made to herself not to mix business with pleasure, she just had. Even though her conscience had woken up in time to stop things going any further, she'd created a conflict of interest that was very much not negligible. As if she simply could not resist the lure of self-sabotage, she'd put everything she'd worked for into jeopardy. Again. She'd let herself down. Again.

This was so bad, she thought, breaking out in a cold sweat as a cab pulled up and she climbed into it. So very, *very* bad. Maybe even terminal. Once more she'd indulged the chemistry that raged whenever they were close, but this time they were no longer two strangers in a bar with nothing to lose. They were colleagues. And she was halfway through a career-defining assignment with *everything* to lose.

But she was not going to go down without a fight. She wasn't going to go down at all if she could help it. She had the entire weekend to think of a way to fix the situation and reset the status quo, and that was precisely what she would do.

Adam did not have a good weekend. So much for the opportunity to recover from his knackering dash across the Atlantic. Despite working his way through the bottle of whisky in the aftermath of Ella's flight from his apartment, sleep eluded him. Every time he closed his eyes, the memory of the kiss crashed into his head. Such heat. Such eagerness. Then such distress and regret, no doubt caused by the fact that with his confession, he'd shifted their relationship from the professional to the personal.

This was why he fought so hard for control, he thought as he tossed and turned in the early hours of Saturday morning. Because without it he was wild and unpredictable, no better than his father, and he knew the devastation such conduct could cause. He'd behaved impulsively. Selfishly. He'd provoked Ella into doing something she'd never have done otherwise.

Extreme exhaustion, bitter resentment that she'd encountered him in such a febrile state and severe sexual frustration blackened his mood over the course of the day, and it did not go unnoticed.

'For God's sake, smile,' Annabel muttered to him at one point during the white-tie charity gala he'd escorted her to. 'No one's going to believe we're madly in love if you insist on looking like thunder.'

He snapped a smile to his face and forced the tension from his jaw, but his mood did not improve. Not even a Sunday spent pouring over a pile of Helberg Holdings data soothed the rumblings of deep unease.

The only moment of respite he had was a phone call from his sister that he received at 6:00 a.m. on Monday, by which time—having yet again woken early and been unable to get back to sleep—he was already showered, dressed and debating whether to wait for his driver to show up at seven or call a cab.

'I thought you'd like to know I was at tech billionaire Luke Broussard's fifth of July bash in Marin County last weekend,' Charley said, packing in the detail as if she thought it would impress him. 'The photos I posted of me wearing one of my designs are already going viral, which is going to be invaluable publicity for my business. Free publicity. Organic publicity. Plus, I picked up four new commissions while I was there. So I've decided to expand my operation.'

Expand her operation? Adam thought with a frown as, ditching the idea of a cab, he entered the kitchen and pressed yet another espresso capsule into the coffee machine. On the back of some pictures and a handful of new commissions? Was that wise? Should he tell her that? Perhaps she was calling for advice. 'Let me take a look.'

He stalked through the apartment to his study while the machine did its thing and sat down at his desk. After switching on his laptop, he pulled up one of the social media sites he knew she used. There were three photos in total, all showing his sister in a dress that was the colour of bronze and looked great, although he was no expert. But it wasn't the dress that had caught his eye. No. What caught his eye and set off great clanging alarm bells in his head was the man she appeared to be dancing with.

Who was none other than his squash buddy and Helberg rival, Cade Landry.

Adam nearly fell off his chair in shock. He hadn't even been aware they knew each other. But Charley was looking up at Cade with such adoration it was blatantly obvious that they now knew each other extremely well indeed, and a wholly unfamiliar protective instinct kicked in. Could the man have deliberately targeted his sister to win the bet? Had he been unable to resist the opportunity to needle Adam in the process?

As an older brother who'd failed his sister before,

Adam felt it his duty to point out these facts. Unsur-prisingly, Charley did not take the news well.

'Are you serious?' she said in response to the rev-elation that he, Cade and Zane had vowed to date one woman only for the summer in order to decide who won Helberg and that she was now part of it.

He told her that he didn't joke about Montague's and tried to explain the situation again, even offering to fix it, but Charley didn't want his help.

'I'm sorry,' he said with a sigh. 'I didn't mean for you to get caught up in this.'

'I need you to release fifty thousand pounds from my trust fund,' she said coolly, ignoring his apology entirely.

Pinching the bridge of his nose and suppressing the guilt, Adam relented. 'I'll speak to the bank.'

The conversation provided distraction for a full half hour. Ruminating on the fact that this could be an ex-cellent place to start trusting his sister—who might lack his commercial experience but, unlike him, had set up her own company, kept it going and sounded as though she knew what she was doing—mopped another ten minutes.

Then it occurred to him that with these photos going viral, Cade had effectively been knocked out of the competition for Helberg. The rules of the bet would force him to stick with Charley, and she'd made it clear that because of it, she didn't want him any-where near her, and this was another brief but pleas-ing diversion.

But he refused to be blindsided like this again—by *anything* date or bet related—so he emailed Maggie with instructions to cultivate contacts at *Blush* magazine. He didn't care how she did it. Bribery using beauty products. The promise of a dozen full page adverts. It was all good to him. But he needed advance warning of any further updates to the site before they went live.

Now, as he sat in the back of his car on the way to his office, staring unseeingly through the blacked-out windows, Ella was back in his head. How was he going to handle seeing her today? The strength of his desire for her remained a concern. It was inappropriate on too many levels to count.

Could he trust himself to control it? Could he be certain that she would do the same? She'd clearly been as horrified as he was by what they'd done—which was encouraging if they were to forget it had happened—but what if she'd had a rethink over the weekend and decided to pursue the chemistry? What if she wanted more?

An icy chill ran down his spine and his chest tightened as if in a vice. More could not happen. It didn't even bear thinking about. For one thing, the recklessness she aroused in him must not be allowed to return. For another, to the world at large, he was still dating Annabel. If he were seen with Ella too—either two-timing both women or ditching one for another—not only would his reputation take a hit and interest in him spike, but he'd also be forfeiting everything that he'd worked so hard to achieve.

Losing Helberg and, by extension, Montague's wasn't an option. He'd waited too long and it meant too much. Who knew when he might get another chance for redemption? This might be his one shot. And as for the reaction of his rivals should he fail, he could virtually see the crowing now. Cade and Zane would be insufferable. He'd never hear the end of it.

Unless, of course, they didn't find out.

As that thought darted through Adam's head, every atom in his body froze. His pulse skipped a beat and his breath caught in his lungs. Was that even possible? It would be if he saw Ella in secret. She'd mentioned she had three weeks' leave coming up. He could match it. Business was winding down for the summer. He was the boss. Besides, he'd dedicated the last four years to restoring the fortunes of the company, working sixteen-hour days seven days a week, and he couldn't remember the last time he'd taken a break. He could take her to his private island in the Caribbean. They'd be unseen and undiscovered there. He could make the travel arrangements himself and ask Annabel to keep a lower profile for a while. Who else would ever need know?

But, no, he thought, shaking his head to rid it of the mad idea. It was out of the question. Secrecy wouldn't address the risk of his control unravelling and the fallout that might ensue. Besides, such subterfuge would be insanely stressful, not to mention cheating. He'd sacrificed far too many of his principles recently to squander what few he had left. He wouldn't compromise his integrity any further. He just had to harness his formidable willpower and focus on the endgame for what was, after all, only another five days.

Although, would it *really* be cheating? *He* knew he wasn't genuinely dating Annabel and, with regards to his conscience, surely that was all that mattered. She'd set the public record straight if required, not that he would trust either Cade or Zane to believe her if it suited them better not to. But even if he *were* to cheat, the end would justify the means. Business could be brutal. Just look at how Cade had gone about targeting Charley. Had he had any qualms about her identity? Adam suspected not.

And how much damage could be done in three short weeks? It wasn't as if Ella would develop expectations he couldn't meet. He could still recall the shudder with which she'd assured him in that bar that she'd never be after anyone's heart, and he didn't think she'd been lying.

So what exactly was he worrying about? If what went on the island stayed on the island, there'd be no repercussions. He had no reason to believe that succumbing to the physical chemistry might lead to anything deeper. It never had before. He would never be tempted to tell Ella the gory details of his journey to CEO. He would never share with her his ugly selfishness as a teen, his guilt, his self-loathing and his desperate need for absolution.

The details of his mother's overdose and his role in it were for his thoughts alone. Quite apart from the visceral horror of it, spilling his guts and leaving them exposed and bleeding for her to pick through would create a dangerous emotional connection that he'd sworn never to create with anyone in case he failed them and destroyed them too.

He couldn't rely on his desire for Ella suddenly disappearing the minute the audit was over. It might have taken him only days to recover from the incident in the cocktail bar bathroom, but she'd been a stranger to him then. This time round, he'd know where to find her. He'd get no peace. He needed to get her out of his system so he could focus on the takeover. He needed to sort it now so he could get through the next week without losing his mind.

It would mean having to come clean about the bet, of course. His integrity might never recover if he took her to the Caribbean under false pretences. There was also every chance he might be forced to talk about Helberg. But for the sake of the audit, he'd have to disclose his interest in the company at some point, so why not now? He wouldn't need to go into detail. He wouldn't be exposing parts of himself that had never seen the light of day. It would be fine.

The key point here was that he wanted her and he wanted Helberg, and with a little deception, some careful planning and a few tricks up his sleeve to neutralise any objections she may raise, he could have both.

CHAPTER SEVEN

ELLA WAS PACKING up her workstation when out of the corner of her eye she saw Adam exiting the lift and striding in her direction. But despite the leap of her pulse and a hot surge of desire, she didn't pause, not even for a second. She'd been preparing for this moment ever since she'd thought of it in the early hours of yesterday morning. They couldn't continue working together in the same space and breathing the same air, she'd concluded as she'd lain in bed, tossing and turning, so stressed by the memory of the kiss that her cortisol levels had to have been sky high. Not after what had happened. The chemistry that still arced between them was simply too dangerous, and she had to put a stop to the self-destruction upon which she appeared hell-bent.

Furthermore, she'd finally succumbed to curiosity and googled his name and had come across a photo of him wrapped round a stunning redheaded supermodel at some charity gala the night before—his *girlfriend* no less, according to one article she'd read yesterday evening, in which the luscious Annabel St James had gushed with excitement about the brand-new love of her life.

Evidently, Adam had lied about always being single that night in the bar, but what did she care? It wasn't as if she were jealous or anything. How dumb would that be? And what would she have to be jealous of anyway? Their relationship? No, thanks. Although it did explain why he'd been so keen to forget their one-night stand. And why he'd been so resolute it was never going to happen again. Why he'd kissed her so thrillingly on Friday night instead of pushing her off wasn't her problem.

It had briefly crossed her mind as she silenced the alarm at six and buried her head beneath her pillow that she could call in sick. She could work from home and avoid having to face the boss she'd thrown herself at so shamelessly. But she'd dismissed the thought virtually the instant it entered her head because she would not be doing any such thing. She was stronger and braver than that, and the success of this job meant far too much. She wouldn't put her promotion in jeopardy just because she felt uncomfortable and it wasn't as if this would be the first time she showed up to work riddled with embarrassment and shame.

When her secret affair with Drew had eventually become public knowledge, she'd run the gauntlet of sly comments and knowing looks. Her private life had suddenly been up for scrutiny, of far more interest than her work, and that had been a situation that no amount of career planning had prepared her for.

The humiliation and loss of respect had been crushing. One of her colleagues, who'd previously openly admired her work ethic, had questioned her career progression, implying that she'd only achieved what she had by lying flat on her back. Another had asked with suspicion whether any indiscreet office banter could have been reported further up the chain.

She'd had to fight damn hard to get over the mortification and restore her colleagues trust in her. It had been months before they'd gossiped in front of her again. Longer still to get to the point where she could be assigned an audit as significant as this one and it didn't raise a single eyebrow. But she'd survived that and she'd survive this too.

'Where do you think you're going?' Adam said, his voice doing strange things to her insides.

'I'm moving downstairs,' she replied, stuffing some papers in a box and looking anywhere but at him because it was too mortifying, too risky, too everything.

'We've already had this discussion.'

Yes, well, a lot had happened since then. But despite the mess she'd made of things—would she *never* learn?—she wasn't going to resign any more than she was going to let him fire her and the plan she'd come up with was the only way forward.

'This arrangement is no longer workable.' She unplugged her laptop and stowed it in her briefcase. 'We clearly can't exist in the same space without some kind of chemical reaction going on. Distance is the only option. It worked last week. It'll work this week.'

'You're running away again.'

So what if she was? The only thing that mattered was completing the audit so she could reboot her career, and that wouldn't happen if she had a constant reminder of what they'd done. 'I'm trying to ensure success.'

'That means a lot to you, doesn't it?'

'What makes you say that?'

'You fight hard.'

'I do. I've had to fight for everything.'

'The three jobs, the trailer, the dead-beat parents, the promotion. I remember. So how did you screw up?'

She wasn't telling him *that*, she thought with a shudder, regretting even more that she'd been goaded into letting that slip on Friday night. Her last disaster of a relationship was not a topic of conversation. It was bad enough *her* knowing she'd made the same mistake twice. If Adam ever found out, he'd probably question her judgement. He might decide she was replaceable even at this late stage in the proceedings.

'Launching myself at you wasn't my wisest move,' she said, deliberately misunderstanding him. 'Please accept my apologies. It was deeply unprofessional. I can't think what came over me. But rest assured that it won't happen again.'

He perched on the edge of the table and folded his arms across the hard muscled chest, against which she'd been plastered for all too brief a moment. 'That's a shame.'

'Why?'

'I don't think much of your solution to our little problem.'

She frowned. 'If you have a better idea,' she said, pretty sure that their problem was anything but little, 'I'd be delighted to hear it.'

'I think we should have an affair.'

At that, Ella's eyes widened and her jaw dropped. What? *What?* On the one hand, it was a huge relief to know that he wasn't planning on firing her for overstepping the line as thoughtlessly as she had, but on the other, what on earth made him think an affair would be a good idea? 'Have you gone stark raving mad?'

'On the contrary,' he said with enviably cool. 'I'm thinking clearly for the first time in a week.'

'Lucky you.'

'This chemistry we share isn't going to go away,' he said far too reasonably given the subject matter. 'The more we've denied it, the more it's returned with a vengeance. Do you really think that out of sight will mean out of mind?'

It had to. It was the only option. 'I'm willing to give it a try.'

'What we *ought* to try is getting it out of our systems.'

Her head began to pound. 'That's the most ridiculous thing I've ever heard of. What if it doesn't work? What if it gets worse?'

'If I remember correctly, you have three weeks'

leave coming up,' he continued, completely ignoring her very valid point. 'So what I'm suggesting is that as soon as the audit is over, we spend your time off doing just that. No lines will be crossed. There will be no conflict of interest. Just sex. And lots of it. For a finite period of time.'

Her heart raced. Her mouth was bone dry. God, this *conversation*. He should not be talking about sex at work. Or anywhere. 'Or we could just say farewell on Friday and that would be that.'

'Is that what you really want to do?' he said with an assessing tilt of his head. 'Remember what we did in the bathroom of a bar, Ella? Imagine what we could do in a bed.'

That was the trouble, she thought a little desperately. She'd spent *hours* over the weekend imagining what they could do in a bed, and she *didn't* want to say farewell on Friday, which was why she was having to use every drop of willpower she possessed to bite back the desperate *yes* that was trying to escape. 'I might have plans.'

'Cancel them.'

If she had had any plans, she would have bristled in response to that diktat. But she didn't. Having bought her own place eighteen months ago and with a pay rise that hadn't materialised, she'd had to rule out travel of any sort this year. And she was bristling about something else anyway. 'And what would your girlfriend have to say about you embarking on a sizzling three-week affair with someone else?'

Adam's dark eyebrows rose for a moment, then lowered. 'Nothing,' he said with a shrug of his impossibly broad shoulders and the glimmer of a smile. 'Because I don't have a girlfriend.'

Ella stared at him. Was that really what he was going with? Denial? How dared he? She well knew how *that* played out for the woman concerned. When Drew had been confronted with the evidence of their affair, he'd blamed it all on her, the rat. How she'd ever believed herself in love with him when he'd just been in it for the sex she had *no* idea. At precisely what point had she forgotten that security came from her career, which she could control—as long as she paid attention—and not a relationship, which she couldn't? Truly, she did not know what she'd been thinking. 'Well, she and the press are under the impression you do.'

Adam's unwavering gaze bore into hers. The intensity of it seemed to be tinged with indecision, and she briefly wondered, was he about to spin her a story? Was he trying to work out whether or not she would believe it?

'The weekend before last, I featured in a magazine article that went viral,' he said with a wince that looked genuine enough, but who knew? 'It focused on the dating habits of myself and a couple of friends, implying that we're all one-date wonders. It wasn't very flattering. It presented a severe risk to my reputation, to the *company's* reputation, and it was generating some extremely inconvenient press and social media attention. Annabel agreed to act as my girlfriend for the summer in order to stop it.'

For a moment, Ella didn't know whether she believed what he'd just told her or not. What with the way this conversation had developed, her brain simply couldn't process it. And once it had—deciding in the end that it was too mad a story to have made up—all she could think to say, was, 'Are you *serious*?'

'Very much so,' he replied coolly. 'I've spent four years clearing out the rot caused by my father and rebuilding the Courtney Collection's brand. I won't let anything jeopardise the progress I've made. Certainly not some two-bit magazine that can't get its facts straight. That's not even who I am any more. If they'd bothered to do their research, they'd have discovered that almost all of the women I appear in public with are in some way involved with the company.'

Yes, well, whether or not he was actually a one-date wonder, she could certainly sympathise with not wanting to jeopardise progress. She'd read about the antics of Edward Courtney—who hadn't?—and occasionally she'd allowed herself to wonder how Adam felt about that, what it could have been like growing up the son of such a man. But what a way to go about it. It seemed like something out of a farce and very much not the behaviour of a controlled CEO of a Fortune 500 company.

Although his kiss hadn't been in the slightest bit controlled, now that she thought about it. It had been hot and wild and desperate, and not a betrayal of anyone, which was *such* a relief, because even though she'd been unaware of this Annabel St James at the time, she'd still felt sickened and ashamed when she'd found out about her, as though she'd trampled all over the sisterhood. 'How long are you planning to keep up the charade?'

'Until Labor Day.'

'That's very specific.'

'There's a bet,' he said easily, as if there was nothing outrageous at all about making such a thing. 'It involves Helberg Holdings. I imagine you've noted that I've been buying up the shares. I intend to take it over, but I'm not the only one after it. There are three of us. My fellow one-date wonders. We each now hold a large stake in it. None of us is prepared to back off. It was proposed that to break the dead lock and shut down the reputational damage caused by the article, we each date one woman between now and Labor Day. Anyone caught dating more than one woman in that time relinquishes their claim on Helberg.'

Once again, he'd rendered her speechless. Ella stood there, staring at him, not quite sure where to start with all that. Then she realised that she had the opportunity to get somewhere with her enquiries, and she was damned if she wasn't going to take it. 'What's your interest in Helberg?' she said, parking her many questions about the bet until later. 'I looked into the company. Its portfolio is huge and in trouble. It seems an odd fit.'

'I'm after Montague's.'

'The international jewellery business?'

How many times had she walked past the flagship store on Fifth Avenue? Only about a thousand. And how many times had she failed to stop and look at the eternally gorgeous window display? None. Even though, these days, the woodwork was peeling and the signage was rusting, the cases behind the glass were always so prettily filled. She had no interest in the engagement, wedding and eternity rings, of course, but she'd always thought a tennis bracelet or a pair of diamond stud earrings might be nice.

'That's the one,' he confirmed with a nod. 'It used to belong to the Courtney Collection. It's been allowed to decline and I want it back. I've waited ten years for the chance, and I won't let anything get in the way of it, whether that's a threat to my reputation, external competition or problems raised by an audit.'

Ah. So that was why he'd been so insistent on keeping such a close eye on things. And, presumably, why he'd been so willing to ignore a potentially pesky conflict of interest or two. But ten years? Buying an entire conglomerate just to acquire one relatively small company? A bet? 'It sounds as though Montague's is more than just business to you.'

Despite his outward languor, a muscle jumped in his cheek. 'It's all about the bottom line.'

'Are you sure it's not a game?'

'It's very much not a game.'

'Yet you've bet on it, which is not only unbelievably puerile but also fails to take into account the agency of the women involved. Plus, you've agreed to terms which make no sense, because what if you all win?'

'That won't happen,' he countered with absolute confidence. 'You don't know Cade Landry and Zane deMarco. They'll be out any time now, if they aren't already. And believe me, I am extremely aware of how puerile it is. And the questionable ethics of involving women. Which is why Annabel is fully appraised of the circumstances and why I'm telling you now. To lay all my cards on the table. So there are no misunderstandings.'

'You're cheating.'

'Not technically.'

Hmm. 'You want me to be your dirty little secret.'

'The dirtier the better.'

'That's shameless.'

'I go for what I want and I want you.' His gaze fixed on her mouth and heat flooded her body. 'Do you have any other objections?'

Well, she *ought* to, she thought, trying the stamp out the desire beginning to thud away inside her. She ought to have plenty. For one thing, she was *not* having another office affair. The last one had caused quite enough trouble. A second would sink her career for good if it came to light. Of course, if it started after Friday, with the audit signed off and Adam no longer her client, it wouldn't actually be an office affair.

But it wasn't a question of semantics. Or that simple. Nor was it just a matter of timing, despite what Adam evidently thought. It had been easy enough to part company five weeks ago, when she'd only known him for twenty minutes, but what if this time round she found it harder? What if once again she lost her head, got to know him and at the end of their time together wanted more? Or *he* did? How would she disentangle herself from that?

And if she *did* agree to an affair, would she really be all right with the subterfuge? She would be tinged with grubbiness—again—even if he had been open and transparent with her, which, come to think of it, perhaps made her feel slightly less grubby and maybe even a little bit flattered because he clearly wanted her enough to risk the company he'd been working so hard to get.

However, she'd been down that road before and she had too much self-respect to travel along it again. Although, she couldn't deny that the discretion would suit her as much him because it wouldn't do her reputation any good to be caught in the company of a man who had so recently been her client, however unlikely that might be.

But, no. Right now, she needed to focus one hundred percent on her career. She couldn't afford to be distracted. Of course, the sex would be dynamite. And the next five days would be a lot easier to handle with the promise of relief at the end of them. Furthermore, with the three-week time frame he'd specified, there'd be a definite end. There'd be no danger of entanglement. There simply wouldn't be time to lose her head. She would never want anything more, with

Adam or anyone, and this limited the risk of that for everyone involved.

Commitment, which seemed to require constant sacrifice and compromise, did not appeal. Even the *thought* of 'settling down' sent chills darting through her and she certainly no intention of ever having children. She'd witnessed first hand how well *that* worked out for women occupying senior positions in her field. At her previous company, one associate director had married, and in the immediate aftermath, some jerk had opened a book on how long it would be before she announced she was pregnant. Ten months, as it happened. Three months after that the same colleague had gone on maternity leave and when she had come back a year later, she'd found that her job wasn't quite what it had been. Somehow she'd become…*lesser*. Respect for her and belief in her ability had plummeted. Eventually, she'd left and was last heard to be working part time at a third rate out-of-state firm.

Ella couldn't even contemplate the thought of unwillingly—or even willingly—giving up everything she'd worked so hard for, and if that made her selfish in the eyes of others, well, she could live with that. She would never want to resent a husband or kids for holding her back. That wouldn't be fair to anyone.

But a hot, purely physical summer fling with a man to whom she was wildly attracted *did* appeal to her. Very much. Getting him out of her system would be a scorching, thrilling rollercoaster of a ride. She couldn't think of a better way to celebrate a successful audit, a promotion and a pay rise. After keeping her nose to the grindstone this last year, she deserved some fun. And so what if she was his dirty little secret? He was hers too.

'Three weeks?' she said, her pulse racing as the last of her resistance crumbled beneath the fizzling pressure of such hot heady desire.

'I don't have the time for anything more.'

'Just sex?'

'No strings. No complications. Just sex.'

'Then I'm all out of objections.'

'Excellent.' A gleam of triumphant satisfaction lit the gorgeous blue depths of his eyes. A devastatingly sexy smile curved his mouth, and as shivers ran up and down her spine, she wondered what on earth she was letting herself in for. 'How do you feel about the Caribbean?'

CHAPTER EIGHT

ELLA ARRIVED AT the exclusive out-of-town airport first thing on Saturday morning as instructed, practically quivering with anticipation. The excitement leaping about inside her was almost impossible to contain.

For one thing, she'd never been to the Caribbean. Generally, when she took a vacation, she went to Europe to improve her knowledge of geography, culture and history, only occasionally venturing farther afield, to India, Africa, Japan. Secondly, the heat in Manhattan in summer could be unbearably stifling, and a balmy private island which would ensure the discretion they both favoured sounded like a delightful alternative. Far more importantly, however, she was now mere hours away from allowing herself to give into the temptation that had plagued her since the moment she'd arrived at the Courtney Collection.

The last five days had not given either her patience or her nerves an easy ride. Evidently flush with success at having secured her agreement to an affair, Adam had persuaded her not to move downstairs. It hadn't taken much. He'd suggested treating the countdown to the end of the week as foreplay, and she was all unpacked three minutes later.

She'd half thought she'd regret the added distraction. But she hadn't, because she'd entered such a state of hyperawareness that the audit had kicked up a gear. Progress had steamed ahead as if on steroids. Long steamy looks across the divide had not derailed it. Nor had conversations that were ostensibly about the methodologies used to value inventory and the whereabouts of documents relating to revenue recognition but at the same time were laden with subtext. Somehow, she'd even managed to rise above the occasional steamy text message he sent.

Where were you at lunchtime?

That was how one such exchange had started.

I went shopping for Caribbean-friendly clothes.

That was a waste of time.

Why?

You won't be needing any.

The audit had wrapped up to her satisfaction, bang on time on Friday afternoon, and she hadn't stuck around to celebrate for long. She'd gone for one quick drink with her team, but she'd been too distracted by her own scorching thoughts to stay.

Now, the car that Adam had sent for her was drawing up to the jet that stood on the tarmac and shone bright white in the early morning sun. The driver opened the rear passenger door and Ella climbed out. Her entire body thrumming with adrenaline, she thanked him and then walked up the steps as if she did this sort of thing all the time. She ducked her head and entered the cabin to find Adam had beaten her to it. He was sitting on a buttoned sofa in a space that—with the low lighting, sumptuous furnishings and highly polished wood décor—looked more like the cocktail bar in which they'd met than any plane she'd ever been on.

Watching her with an intensity that ramped up the thrills whizzing through her to an almost intolerable level, he got to his feet, and immediately the cabin seemed to shrink in size and run out of air.

'Good morning,' she said breathlessly while trying to keep it cool because a crew member was flitting about, so they weren't alone.

'Good morning,' he said, his voice deep, low and tinged with a roughness that made her shiver. 'Come and join me.'

Giddy with the realisation that there was no longer any need to keep her distance, Ella did as he suggested. She walked towards him, feeling as though she were tied to the end of a rope he was slowly hauling in, and when he sat, so did she. The cream leather sofa was comfortable but small. Her knee was inches from his. His intoxicatingly masculine scent instantly

enveloped her, and she fizzed so badly with the need
to touch him that she had to sit on her hands.

'Coffee?'

'Thank you.'

He turned a fraction and leaned forward to pour her
a cup. His shoulder brushed hers as he moved, and she
nearly leapt out of her skin. She was never going to
last the flight if she carried on like this, she thought
despairingly, letting out a long slow breath and willing her heart rate to slow. She had to calm down. She
really did. And what was there to be jittery about anyway? She was being ridiculous.

Mentally giving herself a firm shake, Ella accepted
the cup he offered her with a hand that she was pleased
to see was now as steady as a rock and took a forti-
fying sip.

'How was the show?' she asked, referring to the
Broadway play he'd attended last night with Annabel
and stamping out the voice that was whispering *dirty
little secret* in her ear, because this was nothing like
the illicit affair she'd had with Drew. Adam had been
very clear about what he wanted from her. Exactly
why he too was interested in no strings or complications was irrelevant. They were on the same page.
That was the main thing. And this time round, she
had herself under control. Mostly.

'Interminable,' he replied. 'How were the drinks?'

'Short.'

Even though she could look at him forever, to do
so was sorely testing her resolve. So as the engines

fired, she glanced around, her curiosity piqued, her auditing antennae quivering despite being on leave. 'Is this the company jet?'

'I wouldn't dare.'

Her gaze swung back to his. A gleam lit the blue depths of his eyes. The ghost of a smile played at his mouth, and she wanted to kiss him so badly she ached with it. 'You hired one just for me?'

'I *bought* one just for you.'

For a moment, Ella didn't know what to say. Her brain had completely stalled. She'd never had anyone go to such lengths to address her concerns or want her so much that they bought a plane to facilitate a three-week fling. Drew, who, mortifyingly, had not had to woo her at all because somehow she'd thrown her self-respect out of the window along with her sanity and slept with him the night he'd chatted her up, hadn't even bought her dinner. 'I'm flattered.'

'I'm regretting it doesn't have a bed.'

That was indeed a shame, she thought, swallowing hard in response to the smoulder with which he was looking at her. 'How long is the flight?'

'It's five hours to Aruba. From there, fifteen minutes in a seaplane.'

'I believe it's called delayed gratification,' she said, wondering how on earth she was going to stand it.

'I believe it's called torture.'

'What shall we do to occupy the time?'

'How about I tell you everything I intend to do to you when we land?'

A flush hit her cheeks. Her pulse rate rocketed. Her lungs seemed to have collapsed. 'Will that take five hours?'

'More.'

Oh dear God. 'We have company.'

'Then come closer.'

Helpless to resist, Ella put down her cup and did so. Adam was as good as his word, his level of detail as impressive as it was mind-blowing, and by the time they arrived at the island mid-afternoon, she could barely stand. Her limbs were liquid. Her heart was beating so hard she was surprised she hadn't cracked a rib.

She'd never experienced anything like the intensity of his focus, she thought as she disembarked from the seaplane they'd transferred to in Aruba and he'd piloted himself. For as long as she could remember, she'd been her number one priority. Now she appeared to be someone else's, albeit temporarily, and it was a bit bewildering.

However, she must not let it overwhelm her. She must not allow herself to be swept up in the attention. It would do her no good at all to get carried away by the fairy-tale romance of it all. She was an auditor with a fondness for spreadsheets. Practicality and realism were in her DNA. For all she knew, Adam treated all the women he slept with like this. And what they were doing was about getting him out of her system, not allowing him to work his way even further into it.

While he removed their luggage from the seaplane,

Ella stood on the jetty and surveyed the landscape. To her left, the rocky coastline disappeared around a curve. To her right stretched a band of dazzling pristine white sand upon which lapped tiny crystal-clear waves. Beyond the idyllic beach, nestled among the palm trees, stood the house, a sprawling white two-storey building with a wraparound veranda on the ground floor and balconies on the second supported by elegant white columns.

It was stunning, classy, everything she'd expect from a luxury goods magnate and nothing like what she was used to, and suddenly an unexpected flurry of nerves swooped into her stomach, because what was she doing? This wasn't her world. She wasn't a private-jet-private-island-billionaire's-plaything sort of a person. She ought to be back in New York, man-free, drycleaning her suits and clearing her inbox. This was reckless, rash and—

'Are you all right?'

His voice cut through the rising panic, and she blinked and blew out a breath as her pulse began to slow. There was no need to overthink this. It was a fling. That was all. And hadn't she just told herself not to get carried away? She had to ease up. Focus on the facts. Chill out, as they said, even though she couldn't recall the last time she'd actually done that. 'I'm just taking a moment.'

'Having second thoughts?'

'No.'

'Sure?'

'Yes.'

'Then stop dawdling.'

He slung his bag over his shoulder and picked up her case. With his free hand he took her elbow, then led her along the jetty and up some steps. He propelled her along a wide sandy path that led to the house and in through the front door. He dropped the case and the bag and kicked the door shut.

But she didn't get a chance to check out the light airy space, because in the blink of an eye he'd pushed her up against the wall and slammed his mouth down on hers, instantly wiping her head of the doubts and the nerves, because *this* was what they were about. Chemistry. Sex. Nothing else.

So it didn't matter what he was or what she was. All that mattered was that this was a kiss she'd waited over week for, a kiss that had kept her awake at night, twisting and turning in torment, and it was everything she'd been anticipating. More. It was hot. Wild. Electric. Days of pent-up desire exploding in a clash of teeth and a tangle of tongues.

Dizzy with longing, as tiny bombs of excitement detonating inside her, Ella lifted her hands to his shoulders, tracing the contours of his muscles that bunched and flexed beneath the black cotton of his polo shirt. She dug her fingers in his hair. He held her hips and pulled her pelvis to his so she could feel exactly how badly he wanted her.

His erection pressed hard against her and liquid heat pooled between her legs. Fire rushed through her veins. He tasted and felt better than she remembered and her entire world shrank to him, this dominating, punishing, utterly magnificent kiss and the ferocious need that pulsated between them.

He eventually tore his mouth from hers and she dragged in a much-needed breath, only to lose it again when he turned his attention to her jaw, her earlobe, her neck and the pulse that throbbed wildly at the base of it. When he slid a hand up her side to her breast, cupping it and brushing a thumb over her tight, aching nipple, she gasped in response to the lightning bolt of ecstasy that shot through her. Her knees buckled, and if he hadn't been pinning her to the wall, she'd have collapsed to the floor.

Desperate to arouse the same sensations in him, she disentangled her fingers from his hair and ran them over his hard, muscled chest, down, down, down to the waistband of his jeans—at which point he stilled, lifted his head from her neck and jerked back.

She opened her eyes, suddenly wracked with confusion. 'Why are you stopping?' she panted, gazing helplessly into his darkly glittering eyes.

'I promised you a bed.'

He scooped her up, and before she could protest that she wasn't some faint-hearted damsel in distress, he was carrying her across the hall and up the stairs. He barged into a room and dropped her onto the vast bed. Thinking that, actually, she would play the damsel in distress any day of the week if it meant being enveloped in all that heat and strength, Ella took the opportunity to whip off her sundress and tossed it aside.

Adam came straight down on top of her, and within moments, her bra had joined her dress on the floor. His mouth landed first on one breast, then the other, and as he began to lavish attention on her, she lost all track of time and place. Her head spun and her breath stuck in her lungs. The sensations sizzling through her were so devastatingly powerful, she had to bite her lip to stop herself from crying out.

'There's no one to hear you but me,' he muttered, his hot breath tickling her feverish skin as he began to inch his way down her body. 'Make as much noise as you want.'

When he reached the juncture of her thighs, he deftly removed her underwear. Then he put his mouth on her and she did as he suggested. She couldn't help it. She was beyond reason and he was just too good at this. Gasping, groaning, parting her legs even further, she clutched at the sheet with one hand and kept his head in place with the other. She tried to writhe to alleviate the throbbing ache, but he held her still. He removed her hand from his head, trapping her wrist on the bed, and took full command, dictating the pace, ignoring her pleas and increasing the torment until she was sobbing and begging for release.

She'd never felt desperation like it, never wanted something so badly, and when her orgasm finally hit, it struck with the force of tsunami, drenching her in such pleasure so intense she felt as though she might drown in it.

With stars still exploding in her head, her breathing still ragged and shallow, Adam reared up. He stripped off his clothes and rolled on a condom, and then he was back between her legs, angling her hips and sliding his gloriously thick length into her. And although it did not seem possible—surely her body couldn't recover from something so exceptional so quicky— a fresh wave of desire surged through her.

He kissed her deeply, fiercely, the taste of her on him scattering what few wits she'd managed to gather. When he began to move, she clung to his broad shoulders and wrapped her legs around his waist. His skin was hot and slick. The friction of his hair-roughened chest against hers was sensational. With every slow, controlled thrust, she lost a little bit more of her mind.

And she could tell that he was losing his too. He'd wrenched his mouth from hers and buried his head in her neck. His thrusts were becoming less measured and increasingly frantic. Astonishingly, the exquisite pressure was building inside her again, like a bonfire that had merely been doused, not wholly put out.

She tightened her legs around his hips and dug her fingers into his back, her blood on fire, her breathing rough. Then somehow, he slipped his hand between them, skilfully finding the spot where she pulsed and burned, and she shattered, gasping, panting, crying out his name. A second later, with a muffled roar, he buried himself deep inside her one last time and collapsed.

'Well, that was worth waiting for,' she murmured once she'd regained her breath and he'd lifted his weight off her.

'That's just the start of it,' he muttered raggedly, staring down at her, his glittering gaze filled with promise. 'We have days to make up for, and as you know, my imagination's been hard at work.'

'So's mine,' she said with a delicious little shiver.

'Show me.'

While Ella lay sprawled on the bed beside him, the midnight moonlight giving her skin a silvery glow, Adam reflected that she had been bang on with her observation about delayed gratification.

The last week in the office had been insanely tough. Never had his self-control been so tested. He lost count of the number of times he'd been forced to remind himself of his commitment to the bet and the significance of the audit for his takeover in order to stop himself from buckling beneath the overwhelming crush of desire and taking her where she sat. And he'd evidently developed masochistic tendencies, because he could have drummed up any number of meetings to spare himself the torment of having her constantly in his line of sight, but he hadn't. He could also have let her move downstairs as she'd wished, but he hadn't done that either.

So much for the assumption that arranging an affair would ease what remained of the audit, he'd thought every time he'd stepped into the shower and flipped the dial to cold. In practice, the unbearable week had crawled by so slowly it had frequently felt as though time were going backwards. The plane ride down here, during which he'd let his imagination run riot and caused himself a whole lot of pain in the process, had seemed to last years instead of hours.

And yet he'd undergo every single second of it all over again if it meant the kind of sex they'd spent the afternoon having. What they'd got up to had far surpassed anything his feeble imagination had managed to conjure up. One minute it was feverish, frantic and explosive. The next it was slow and thorough, though nonetheless earth-shattering. There was barely an inch of her he hadn't explored at length, and she'd spent a good hour tormenting him with her hands, mouth and hair while he simply lay back and surrendered. Her insatiability—and his—would be the death of him. Not even in his wildest days as a reckless teenager had he lost it so hard and so often. And best of all, they had an entire three weeks of it.

The intensity of the experience was greater than he'd been expecting. Greater than anything he'd come across before, in fact. But he had no doubt that it would soon fade. It invariably did. And most likely it was caused by a five-day run-up that had been as hot as it could be without physical contact anyway.

Nor was he overly concerned by the efforts he'd made to arrange the affair. Practically speaking, all he'd had to do was make some calls and get out his cheque-book. Annabel, who'd been intending to spend the summer at an Austrian health retreat before he'd asked her to escort him around the city, had had no problem reviving that plan. It was the work of a moment to instruct the house to be opened up and another couple of hours to purchase the plane.

Telling Ella about the bet had not been difficult either. He wasn't remotely concerned he wouldn't win it, despite what she'd said. He'd briefly checked out the *Blush* magazine website for the latest tally, and it was true that Cade and Zane had gone rather quiet on the dating front, but it was early days.

Furthermore, as he'd suspected, revealing the bare bones of his interest in Helberg had been fine too. She hadn't pushed him further on why Montague's was so important to him, which would certainly have been a trickier conversation to navigate, so on the whole, he was extremely satisfied with how everything had played out. And there was no denying that a plane for personal use would come in handy once the takeover was complete and he had more time on his hands.

The only thing he didn't much like was the fact that she believed herself to be his dirty little secret. Despite the planning he'd done, he'd failed to consider the possibility she might think that. It disturbed his already compromised principles and left the hint of a bitter taste in his mouth. But if she could get over it, then so could he.

The crucial thing was that they were singing from the same hymn sheet. They were both in this just for

the sex. Why that was important to her didn't matter.
All he needed to know about her was which position
she fancied trying next.

CHAPTER NINE

SEVERAL DAYS LATER, although quite how many she couldn't be sure because she'd lost all sense of time and space, Ella woke late in the afternoon to an empty bed and the sound of the shower being switched off.

What a time she and Adam had been having, she thought with a languid stretch that eased the delightful ache in her muscles. There'd been so much sex. So much pleasure. He'd followed through on every one of the promises he'd made to her on the plane and she was delighted and relieved she'd suppressed her misgivings and agreed to come. She could not get enough of him. Which perhaps didn't bode all that well for getting him out of her system, but this fling of theirs was still in its infancy.

With desire once again fluttering, Ella was wondering what was taking him so long when her phone beeped to alert her to an incoming email. Lazily, she rolled over and picked up the device. She unlocked it and opened the app—and sat bolt upright when she saw that the message was from her boss.

For a moment, she didn't dare click on it, because

this one message held her entire future in its hands. She thought the audit had gone well, but what if it hadn't? What if something had gone wrong? What if somehow the conflict of interest she and Adam had both been so keen to ignore had been uncovered, the audit rendered invalid, and she was being fired?

Ella swallowed hard and pulled herself together. She took a deep breath and shook the tension from her shoulders. She was being ridiculous. Why would something have gone wrong?

Nevertheless, her stomach was tumbling and her chest was tight as she opened the email. With her heart in her mouth, she read it once, twice, a third time—and then punched the air in triumph, because she'd done it. She'd actually done it. The promotion was hers. All that hard work had paid off. She was back in from the cold with a twenty percent pay rise and assigned to a great big fat audit starting in September. Her career was back on track. Her future was secure. She could finally put the last horrible year behind her and move on. And, God, it was a *relief*, because she could now admit that she'd been more than a little nervous waiting for the verdict.

'You look happy,' said Adam, walking into the room, naked but for a towel around his waist and another around his neck.

Ella broke off the victory dance she was doing on the bed and beamed at him. 'I just got that promotion I was after.'

She thought she saw a tiny frown crease his brow,

but it was there and gone so fast she realised it must have been a trick of the light. 'Congratulations.'

'Thank you,' she said, flopping back against the pillows and admiring his broad, hard chest, which was glistening alluringly with water droplets. 'I can't tell you how relieved I am. It's been long overdue.'

He pulled the towel from his neck and began to rub his hair dry. 'I remember you saying you screwed up. What happened?'

Ella stilled for a second, the bubble of happiness bouncing around inside her deflating a fraction, because, damn, that had been careless. She'd inadvertently piqued his interest, and now she was in a spot because there were only two ways in which to respond—prevarication or confession.

Since she abhorred the first—to her it seemed not only weak but also a monumental waste of time—that only left the second. Which, most likely, meant telling him everything that had happened, everything she'd been through, when the whole sorry episode was behind her and she had no intention of ever thinking of it again. Because would he be satisfied with a dismissive wave of the hand and a vague muttering about 'stuff'? She didn't think so. He was all about the minutiae. Some responses to her emails during the audit, she recalled, had run to pages.

Quite honestly, the thought of reliving the ill-judged affair with Drew brought her out in a cold sweat. She'd never shared the full story with anyone. Not even her friends knew all the details. Admitting how stupid she'd been and exposing her fallibility to a supremely confident man like Adam, a man who'd likely never put a foot wrong in his life, appealed even less.

But on the other hand, what if it *wasn't* so easy to move on? What if, despite the promotion that suggested she'd been forgiven, the memories of it continued to hound her, riddling her with doubt and colouring her every decision? How would she stand it?

Maybe she had to offload everything once and for all—the facts, the fallout, the lasting impact the affair had had on her—so she could truly let it go. Maybe it would be cathartic. And as for exposing her fallibility to this man in particular, well, he had no sway over her career any longer. He posed no threat to anything, and she certainly didn't care about his opinion of her. In two and a half weeks' time she'd never even see him again. How bad could it possibly be?

Nevertheless, bracing herself to be hit with a flurry of unpleasant memories and a surge of turbulent emotion, Ella sat up and hugged a pillow to her like some sort of shield. 'Drew Taylor,' she said on a sigh. 'He's what happened.'

'Who's Drew Taylor?'

'A year ago, he was my then boss's then boss. He's also the biggest mistake of my life.'

Adam stilled mid-rub, and while she appreciated the pose that displayed his muscles to their finest advantage, she was more intrigued by the unexpected flare of emotion she saw in his glare when her gaze met his. 'What did he do?'

'Plenty,' she said with a wince and a shudder as she fought to keep the details from flooding her head. 'But then, so did I. I had an affair with him. I knew it was against company policy, but I went ahead with it anyway. For a whole six weeks.'

His eyebrows shot up. 'You did *what*?'

'There's no need for you to be so judgemental about it,' she said, bristling a little even though his incredulity was perfectly understandable and not nearly as great as her own. 'Believe me, I have berated myself repeatedly for it. Barely a day goes by that I don't regret my stupidity.'

Adam abandoned the towel with which he'd been rubbing his head and sat at the end of the bed, facing her. 'I'm not being judgemental,' he said, his expression softening a fraction. 'I'm just staggered that you'd risk your career like that when it obviously matters a great deal to you.'

Yes, well, quite. How very perceptive of him. 'It was an extremely stressful time,' she said, not entirely sure who she was trying to convince most. 'I'd been working long hours and was running on fumes. We were out celebrating the end of a successful financial year, and one thing led to another.' She sighed again. 'To be honest, I'm not sure what I was thinking at the time. I must have been out of my mind. I don't even do relationships. But somehow I got tangled up in it. He was very dynamic. Very persuasive. But I still should have resisted.'

The frown returned. 'Did he take advantage of you?'

'No.'

'It sounds as though he did.'

'I was a very willing participant. Too willing, as it turned out.'

'What do you mean?'

Even though she was beginning to die a little on the inside at the thought of revealing things that were so personal, so ridiculously sentimental, Ella soldiered on because there was no going back now. 'I thought I was in love, which I wasn't, but still. There was definitely some infatuation going on. For him, though, it could not have been more casual. We could not have been more at odds in terms of expectations. And so when we were found out, he threw me under the bus.'

'How?'

'He claimed I'd seduced him and that I wouldn't take no for an answer.'

For a moment there was utter silence. While she'd been speaking, Adam's expression had grown increasingly stony, and by the time she finished, his scowl could have vaporised rock. 'He deserves to be ruined.'

'He does,' she agreed, something deep in her chest twanging in response to his support, which she didn't need but for some reason felt nice to have nonetheless. 'Instead, he got promoted, I got blacklisted. The night you and I met in that bar, I'd just found out he'd been nominated for an award, while I was still battling to repair my reputation. It felt grossly unfair.'

'It's more than grossly unfair,' he said, his jaw now

so tight it looked as if it were about to shatter. 'It's immoral, if not downright illegal.'

'I know.'

'I should fire them.'

Her eyes widened with alarm. 'Please do not do that. They might blame it on me and take my promotion away.'

'All right,' he conceded grudgingly. 'But the minute our contract comes up for renewal, the gloves are off.'

'There's really no need. I can fight my own battles.'

'I wouldn't be doing it for you. I'd be doing it for me. There's no place for misogyny and harassment in any of the Courtney Collection's dealings. There was enough of that going on under my father's tenure.'

'So I've read,' she said, stifling a shudder at the thought of Edward Courtney, who sounded as though he'd been an utterly abhorrent individual.

'So, because of the affair, your career stalled,' he said, bringing the conversation back to the point. 'What other impact did it have?'

'You mean apart from the realisation that I'd recklessly jettisoned the rules I'd lived by for a decade and put my whole career on the line? The humiliation and the shame and the sickening knowledge that I'd badly let myself down? The battering of my self-esteem and my confidence and losing the trust and respect of my colleagues? Nope. I think that's about it.'

Some undefinable emotion flitted across his face. 'Why didn't you leave?'

'Imagine the reference.'

'Did you think about taking the company to court?'

'Only briefly. I couldn't prove anything. And I doubt it would have done my reputation any good, even if I could. Instead, I kept my head down and bided my time until I was given the chance to prove myself. Your audit was it, which was why I was so determined to see it through. Why I repeatedly compromised my principles to make that happen, which didn't feel right when I've always done everything by the book. But I wanted redemption more. I wanted what I deserved.'

'And you got it.'

'I did. Despite my own attempts to sabotage things. I mean, I'd sworn not to mix business with pleasure ever again, and I was determined not to let the attraction I felt for you get the better of me, but I still threw myself at you the evening I confronted you at your apartment. Lately, I really seem to have been my own worst enemy.'

'I provoked you into it.'

'Perhaps,' she agreed, recalling the havoc he'd unleashed in her with his admission that he was as at the mercy of the chemistry that sizzled between them as she was. 'But I'm okay with owning my mistakes. I've always thought it important to learn from them so as not make the same ones again. Obviously, that's something I still need to work on.'

Adam appeared to have no further response to that. He seemed to be waging some sort of war with himself. His fists were clenched, and he looked as though he were ready to rip things apart with his bare hands.

But however soft and warm it made her feel, she really didn't need his outrage. Nor did she want it. In fact, the conversation had turned somewhat darker and heavier than she'd intended, and she was filled with the sudden urge to lighten it.

'Anyway,' she said with a deliberately bright smile, now focused on putting an end to the conversation before it got any more complicated. 'All's well that ends well, and you're now sleeping with a director. So what do you think of that?'

Adam thought so many things about what Ella had just told him he didn't know where to start. When he'd walked into the bedroom and seen her jumping around on the bed and beaming from ear to ear, for a split second he'd thought it was because she was pleased to see him. But that had not been the case. Which was a relief, naturally, because the last thing he wanted was to be responsible for her happiness. The quick tightening of his chest had been caused by indigestion, he was sure.

Her delight at her success had been infectious, and he'd experienced a moment of what might or might not have been pride because he knew how bloody hard she'd worked for it. He'd witnessed it. However, when she'd explained the circumstances surrounding it, those positives had swiftly morphed into a more volatile combination of emotions. Astonishment. Disbelief. And then fury, directed first at the jerk who'd messed her around and then at the company that had treated her so unfairly.

For the first time in his life, he wanted to punch something. Ella's dynamic and persuasive ex specifically, the mere thought of whom made him feel as though he'd swallowed a bucket of battery acid. This Drew Taylor should never have abused his seniority by starting something with her, even if she had been a willing participant. And then to wash his hands of her? What sort of a cowardly bastard did that?

At the very least, the guy deserved to be fired. A couple of phone calls was all it would take, and his career would be history. And once that was done, Adam would then set about taking apart the company she worked for piece by piece. The world did not need businesses with values like that. What she'd been through brought back unpleasant memories of the accusations of sexual harassment made against his father. Of the one member of staff who'd dared to sue and been so thoroughly destroyed by the process she'd never worked again. She'd been living in a hostel, broke and broken, when Adam finally tracked her down in order to reverse the miscarriage of justice at least a little. So unfortunately Ella had probably been right to question the wisdom of such a course of action.

No wonder she'd gone to such lengths to keep the audit on track and trouble-free. She was righting a wrong. Just as he was. But he had to cool it before he burst a blood vessel. He wasn't her avenger and she'd made it clear that she didn't need one. He had enough on his plate with the Helberg takeover. He didn't need to fight for justice on any other playing field. That wasn't what this was about anyway. And if she wanted to carry on working for a company that treated her so badly, that was her business.

So, deploying steely determination, Adam pushed the emotions back into the cage where they belonged and fought the clamouring urge to tell her about the challenges *he'd* faced at work, particularly when he'd taken over as CEO. About how he didn't do relationships either. About Montague's and the reason why he'd let the conflicts of interest they'd had slide.

If she wanted to share details of her past with him, that was up to her. He was under no obligation to reciprocate. And he mustn't. Because losing control physically was one thing. Losing control of his defence mechanisms that kept everyone at arm's length was quite another.

'I'll get the champagne.'

Although it pained her to admit it, a week into their affair, the frustration that Ella had experienced during the first half of the audit returned, and for a very similar reason, namely avoidance. Not when it came to sex. That was more torrid than ever. The afternoon she'd received her promotion, which they'd celebrated not just with champagne but also sex so wild and free she'd given him an orgasm that for one tiny nanosecond had actually made him lose consciousness. Ever since then, he'd been trying to do the same to her, and although he hadn't yet succeeded, his diligence had been thrilling. So no. She had no cause for complaint there. The area that was giving her grief was conversation. Or rather, the lack of it.

By definition, that was a two-way street, but currently most of the traffic was on her side of the road. While she wasn't expecting—and did not particularly want—an in-depth discussion about hope and dreams, she was interested in *slightly* more than just the basic facts about the man she was sleeping with. It was unnerving to know every inch of his body but so little of his mind, other than he had a thing about justice. It didn't feel quite right. But every time she asked him a question that ventured into the vaguely personal, he batted it away or turned the conversation back to her. When that didn't work and she persisted, he distracted her with sex.

'Our trailer park was located in California only a few miles from a swanky golf course and polo field,' she told him one morning in bed in response to his enquiry into how hard she'd had to fight for what she'd achieved. 'It was illegal. And feral. The dogs. The kids. The adults. People who weren't drinking themselves into oblivion were shooting up. We had no air-conditioning and undrinkable water. The plumbing would go down for weeks at a time, and toxic smoke from the nearby dump regularly drifted in through the broken windows.'

'How did you escape?' he asked, propping himself up on his elbow and lazily trailing his fingers over the contours of her body as if mapping her.

'It was tough. My parents dealt drugs to make ends meet. Hard ones, although they were never prosecuted because the cops tended to steer clear of the whole place. I could have easily gone down the same route. Most kids did. But even at an early age, I got the feeling that there had to be something better out there. I don't know why. Maybe I saw something on TV. Anyway, I got myself to high school, where I discovered I had an affinity for numbers and decided that accounting would become my route out. The one good teacher I had told me about charities that would help, and they did. I worked hard to catch up and got the grades. I went for days on end on only three hours' sleep a night, but it was definitely worth the pain. I graduated first in my class at college. Not that that was the end of it, of course. I had to lose the accent. I also had to learn how to read a room and network and educate myself on which fork to use, which actually was quite interesting. Did you know there was a separate plate for salad?'

'Yes.'

'And that it's generally acceptable to eat asparagus with your fingers?'

'I've never eaten it any other way.'

'No, well, you and I couldn't be more different, could we?'

He stilled for a moment, shifted minutely as if to

make himself more comfortable and then resumed his idle exploration of her. 'Do you still see your parents?'

'Not for a decade.'

'Do you mind about that?'

'God, no,' she said with a shudder. 'I can barely believe we're related and I'm very happy relying on myself. I've been doing it for years. I can't ever imagine not. They could be dead, for all I know. I really don't care.'

'You're very tough.'

He sounded impressed and a warm tingly feeling that had nothing to do with desire beginning to wind through her. 'I've had no choice,' she said, ruthlessly stamping it out. 'Once I decided to reject the life that could have been mine, it was the only option. It's been quite a journey and not an easy one, but I don't regret a moment of it. Apart from my one reckless affair, obviously. That was a bad career move. So, what about you? Where did you grow up? What was your home environment like? I've read about your father. It couldn't have been easy.'

But she didn't get an answer. His gaze that was on hers darkened and intensified and her pulse began to pound. 'I think that's best saved for another time,' he murmured suggestively, and before she could protest, he rolled on top of her and silenced her with his mouth.

He kissed her until her head emptied of everything but him. He caressed her breasts, with which he'd developed something of an obsession, and she lost what little was left of her mind. Then, when he finally stopped ignoring her desperate pleas for release and thrust hard into her, there was nothing but fierce heat, ragged breathing and the slickness of their bodies moving together. He was in no hurry. In fact, he seemed to be intent on tormenting her. He drove her to the brink and then pulled her back so often it felt like punishment. When he eventually allowed her to fall apart in his arms, she saw stars for a full five minutes.

This happened again when she tried to find out more about his sister and their relationship. And again when she recalled him telling her that the magazine article was inaccurate because that depiction of him wasn't who he was any more.

It was more than a coincidence, she felt. Just like during the first week of the audit, she suspected he was doing whatever he could to avoid her more challenging questions, and in spite of the pleasure he gave her on these occasions, the imbalance of the situation was becoming a problem. At least for her. It felt like an insult. It felt transactional, and it reminded her too much of her relationship with Drew, who, because he'd been less invested in her than she had in him, had held all the cards.

This was meant to be a meeting of equals, body and mind, and it wasn't. Knowledge was power and Adam had all of it, and it had now reached the point that this state of affairs had to be addressed.

'Do you realise that it's been a week since we got here, and you haven't told me one single significant thing about yourself?' she said over a supper of grilled spiced fish and a mango and avocado salad that had been prepared by the housekeeper who lived on the island but she'd yet to meet. 'Whenever I try to engage you in a conversation about you or anything even in the slightest bit personal, you distract me with sex.'

Adam glanced up from his plate. The flickering candlelight cast dancing shadows over the sharp planes of his face. His expression was unreadable, but his eyes twitched and a muscle jumped in his jaw. 'How is that a problem? Are you bored?'

'Of the sex? No,' she said, while thinking, *As if.* He was keeping her extremely well occupied with sex that was varied and inventive. But that was partly the trouble. 'It's just that it makes me feel as though I'm nothing more than an object of pleasure.'

He frowned and put down his fork. 'I understood you were on board with this being purely physical.'

'I am. To a degree. But I would like to know a bit more about the man I'm sleeping with. I would like some respect. I've told you a lot about myself these last few days yet have had zero in return. It makes me uneasy. I can't help wondering what you have to hide.'

'I don't have anything to hide,' he said smoothly, although tension was beginning to radiate off him in waves. 'Perhaps it's simply that I value my privacy. Perhaps I don't like talking about myself. I never asked you to tell me anything, Ella. I'm under no obligation to reciprocate. This is nothing more than a three-week fling. Don't make it something it isn't.'

At that, Ella's eyes narrowed and her hackles went up. What was he suggesting? That she'd weakened and was now after some sort of relationship with him? Heaven forbid. She was perfectly happy with no strings and no pressure. She always had been. Emotional intimacy was not, and never would be, required.

Yet it struck her suddenly that that was precisely what would happen if she pursued her avid interest in him. She'd be creating a connection that went way beyond the physical. She might start feeling things for him she didn't not want to feel. What if warm and tingly became the norm? What if she developed the urge to rush to *his* defence? She might find herself wanting to extend this affair. Getting involved. Losing her focus. And she needed none of that.

Despite the heat of the evening, an ice-cold shiver race down her spine. Her head swam for a moment and her lungs squeezed. Thank God he'd alerted her to what was going on before she travelled too far down that dangerous path, she thought, drawing in a slow steady breath to ease the quick flare of panic. She hadn't recognised what was going on because it had never happened before, but she did now.

So going forward, she would back right off. She would respect his wishes and protect her own. She would not succumb to such weakness again. She would not allow him to damage her self-esteem when she'd only just recovered it. She would focus on getting him out of her system and nothing else.

'You know what?' she said, not wanting to even

think about how close she'd come to forgetting her number one goal when it came to men—to keep it casual. 'You're absolutely right.'

CHAPTER TEN

ADAM KNEW HE was right. What was going on here was just sex, nothing more, and he'd made that perfectly clear. So when Ella finally stopped trying to get him to talk, he ought to have been delighted. It was exactly what he wanted. It was alarming enough that the desire he had for her remained so strong. But the thought of developing some sort of rapport with her that might lead to emotion of the unpredictable kind brought him out in hives, and he'd been in danger of becoming far too interested in her anyway.

At what point precisely had he stopped trying to maintain his indifference? he wondered as he sat on the terrace with a bottle of beer two evenings later and stared out to sea while she slept inside. When she'd told him about her upbringing? That had certainly shaken him up. He couldn't imagine the poverty and despair of it. Materially, he'd grown up with every privilege going—two roofs over his head, more money in the bank than he could count, a first-class education that had swept him from the country's top boarding schools to Cambridge. She'd had nothing.

Less than nothing. Yet she'd pulled herself up through sheer grit and determination, and he couldn't deny he was in awe of her for it. The night they'd met and she'd dispatched her lecherous fan with a knee to the groin, he'd thought her magnificent and beautiful and fierce, and he still did. He was even impressed by the tenacity that had caused him so much trouble while they'd been working together.

But he didn't need to admire her. He didn't need to think anything about her. Or identify with her ambition and her burning drive to succeed. Wondering what else they might share apart from a non-existent family support network was not required. The fact that they weren't as different as she believed was irrelevant. So in theory, the fact that she'd backed off was a win.

However, bizarrely, he wasn't at all pleased by the withdrawal of her attention. Because she didn't just stop trying to poke around in his psyche. She pretty much stopped talking altogether, and only when it was denied him did he realise that somehow he'd got used to her telling him all about herself. He'd found himself looking forward to their conversations, wondering what she might reveal next, on tenterhooks for any titbit she gave him.

Her sudden disengagement therefore left him feeling slightly flat. The sex, while still as frequent as ever, had become a little—how could he put it?—*soulless*. There was a ripple of tension between them, and the whole point of having an affair in the first place was to clear the air of that.

He couldn't shake her accusation of disrespect. Or the recollection that by her own admission, her previous affair had knocked her self-esteem. Her comment about feeling like an object of pleasure troubled him deeply, even though no-strings sex had always been the deal. He'd found himself dwelling on it and analysing his previous interactions with women, which rarely went beyond one or two nights and never more than a week. Had he distracted them with sex too? Very probably, although it had never given him cause for concern. But somehow this was different. With Ella, such a strategy made him feel queasy. He wasn't entirely sure why.

All he knew was that they didn't seem to be on the same page any more, and that was disturbing. So rectifying the problem became his number one priority. He needed to re-establish control. He needed to put the passion back into the sex and show that he did respect her.

After drumming up and discarding a number of ideas, he eventually, reluctantly, had to accept that just one would work. However much he might loathe the thought of it, he had to give her what she wanted. At least, in part. Only then, he felt, would the equilibrium be restored and the affair back on track.

Surely there were *some* things about him that wouldn't be dangerous to share? Would the sky fall in if he revealed where he'd grown up and a few basic facts about his family? He needn't go deep. And he needn't worry about any consequences. Once this fling was over and she was out of his life for good, he could forget he'd ever said anything. Nothing he told her would go any further. He didn't know whether he could trust her to keep his confidences, but before the audit had started she'd signed an NDA. Did that still apply?

Nevertheless, if he was going to do this—even just a little bit—a change of scenery might be sensible. So far they hadn't left the confines of the villa. The furthest they'd ventured was the beach. Talking to her while enveloped in the intimacy of a bedroom felt unwise. Emotional nudity combined with physical nudity could lead to complications he really didn't need. Therefore, preventative action was required.

Somehow managing to ignore how invitingly tousled Ella looked roused from sleep, the next morning, Adam got her up and out of bed and into his open top jeep for a tour of the island.

He reminded himself to keep his attention on the wide sandy track that followed the 150-acre island's coastline and not on her in her tiny denim hotpants and vest top beneath which she didn't appear to be wearing a bra, and off they set in a cloud of sand and dust.

'You'll note that this is an incredibly beautiful dot on the map,' he said in an opening gambit as he steered the jeep round a bend in the track that took them deeper into the vegetation and obscured more of the cloudless blue sky. 'That's why I bought it. As a place to escape the city and relax. I've had it for a couple of years now. But unfortunately, I don't get here as often as I'd like.'

'No, well, I imagine you're busy,' was all she murmured in response, giving him a cool smile before turning to look at the flora.

He tried again. 'Is this your first time to the Caribbean?'

'Yes.'

'Where do you usually vacation?'

'Europe.'

'Have you ever been to London?'

'Once.'

'That's where I grew up.' He paused to navigate some gnarly tree roots while she bounced around beside him. 'Well, between there and Northumberland on the northeast coast of the country. The family has a castle that sits in the middle of a three-thousand-acre estate, complete with turrets, arrow-slit windows and flying buttresses. Parts of it date back to the twelfth century. All of it is damp and draughty.'

'I can imagine.'

'The Holland Park mansion, on the other hand, has four storeys and looks like a wedding cake.'

'How delightful,' she murmured, grabbing top of the door while he swerved to avoid a rock.

'My family can trace its history to William the Conqueror,' he continued doggedly. 'One of my ancestors was at the signing of the Magna Carta. Another was a courtier to Henry the Eighth. He managed to keep his head. I've no idea how.'

'Well, we all lose our heads sometimes.'

As the greenery thinned and the track curved to once again hug the shore, Adam wiped a bead of sweat from his brow that had nothing to do with the heat and thought that he was certainly losing his. This wasn't working out quite as he'd planned. Her ultra-brief responses to his revelations about where he'd been brought up weren't encouraging. But now that he thought about it, mansions and castles were a pretty insensitive topic of conversation when she'd been raised in poverty in a trailer park. And as for all the talk of his ancestry, who'd be interested in that?

'What do you do in your spare time?' he asked, trying a different tack as they drove past the boathouse that stored wind surfs, a couple of single sculls and other water sports paraphernalia.

'I don't have any spare time.'

A moment later, he pointed to a low white building that had magenta bougainvillea clambering all over it. 'In that cottage,' he said, 'live the caretaking couple who keep the house stocked when I'm here and an eye on the place in my absence.'

'It's charming.'

Disappointingly, she showed as much interest in the rest of the island's sights as she did in his conversation, but Adam remained undeterred. He'd caused this breakdown in communication. It was therefore

up to him to repair it. So the following day, he took
her up in his seaplane in the hope that the stunning
scenery would aid his cause.

Who could fail to marvel at the beautiful sparkling
jade waters, dotted with yachts and water sports afi-
cionados? The islands, some of which were tiny but
mountainous, some of which barely rose above sea
level but spread out for miles? Who could remain
unimpressed by the star-studded resorts, the virgin
beaches or even the Caribbean's largest shipwreck,
which rested nearby in a mere sixty feet of water?

Ella.

That was who.

Just as when he'd taken her on a tour of his property, her enthusiasm for everything was muted. She
expressed polite interest in what he had to show her,
but at the same time, she remained aloof. She wasn't
even moved by the pod of dolphins frolicking around
a catamaran.

It was as if she'd sort of switched off. The more
he tried to get her to engage, the more she withdrew.

'Why are you going to so much effort to show me
around?' she asked at one point as they floated on
the surface of a giant blue hole. 'I thought you valued
your privacy.' The glance she slid him was cool, and
her voice, when she turned his own words back on
him, was dry. 'I hope you're not making this something it isn't.'

The constant brush-offs were frustrating. He was
getting nowhere. The prospect of injecting the pas-

sion back into the bedroom was retreating with every passing hour, and that was alarming. He wasn't used to failure, yet to his consternation, that was precisely what seemed to be happening.

However, defeat was not an option. It never had been, never would be. Not when it came to turning his life around after his mother's death. Not when it came to restoring the fortunes of his company after his father's. And definitely not when it came to acquiring Helberg Holdings, reclaiming Montague's and finding redemption.

Unbending Ella so that their last week together was as good as the first would not be the project to beat him, he vowed. He was in control here, not her. He would break through her defences. He would close the distance between them and put the heat back into the sex. Even if it meant having to tell her more. Even if it meant having to tell her everything.

CHAPTER ELEVEN

ELLA HAD BEEN finding it almost impossible to remain cool and detached when the snippets of information Adam had shared with her were so fascinating and everything he'd shown her was so stunning.

Really, she should have resisted the tour of his island. But he'd taken her by surprise. Up until then, they'd stuck to the villa, so why the sudden change in routine? For a moment she'd wondered whether *he* could be getting bored of *her*. Perhaps she needed to up her game sexwise, she'd thought with a flicker of concern. Unlike him, she didn't have many skills in her repertoire. She was more about numbers than tricks. How might one go about sourcing a pair of handcuffs while languishing incognito on an island that was a fifteen-minute seaplane ride from the nearest shop?

But whatever the reason for the volte-face, she'd figured her body could do with a break. Besides, it wasn't as if she would be making make the mistake of fixating on him again or expressing any great fascination for anything. She'd learned her lesson on that front. She was like a fortress. Rock solid and unassailable.

She'd just about held it together outwardly, but pretty much the minute they'd set off in his jeep for the tour, she'd been captivated by the landscape—the verdancy, the crimson hibiscus that flourished everywhere, the cacti, the palm trees and the sand, so much sand. Her senses had been overwhelmed. The colours were so intense. The sounds so exotic. The scents so deliciously tropical.

When he'd begun to talk, it hadn't taken long for her curiosity to break free of its confines and batter her with the desire to know more. About life in the castle, the wedding-cake mansion and his ancestry. About the staff who worked for him, the rowing boats and how he relaxed. All of it was wildly different to anything she'd ever known. His life experiences had clearly been the polar opposite of hers, which made them all the more gripping.

Then he'd taken her up in the seaplane and dazzled her with sights so stunning she'd wanted to weep. Nature had never looked so majestic. The fact that she'd always overlooked this part of the world seemed unfathomable. What made a blue hole? she couldn't help but wonder. What was the story behind the shipwreck? Did any of the super glamorous resorts belong to him?

However, she'd pushed away these clamouring questions and reined in her curiosity. She'd repeatedly reminded herself of the need to steer clear of any sort of emotional connection with him, to resist getting caught up in the fantastical luxury of it all, and told herself that there was always the internet for the facts.

It was a challenge. The tension generated by such self-restraint was excruciating. But she stayed strong and held off.

Until the night he insisted on joining her for a walk along the beach that she'd planned to take alone to clear her head and strengthen her defences, after a dinner during which he'd seemed distant and preoccupied.

Something was on his mind, she thought, too on edge with awareness and anxiety to fully appreciate the beauty of the dark sea sparkling in the moonlight and the tiny waves lapping gently on the shore. The sand was warm between her toes. The evening breeze caressed the bare skin of her arms and legs.

Peace and tranquillity abounded, but nevertheless her stomach churned and her throat was tight. These past couple of days she'd sensed that he didn't appreciate her lack of engagement, even though he ought to. That was exactly what he'd wanted, wasn't it? So had he had enough? Was she out of his system and was he planning to end the affair? How would she feel if he did? Short-changed? Relieved? She didn't know.

'Let's sit,' he said quietly, cutting through her jittery thoughts and making her jump.

She swallowed hard and fought back the panic which revealed that she *didn't* want this to be over just yet. 'I'd rather be heading back.'

'Please.'

Something about the tone of his voice prickled her skin and switched her senses to high alert. Her heart began to thud. He looked oddly nervous, which was bizarre when she'd never seen him anything other than supremely confident. But at least that ruled out ending things. If that was his intention, he'd come right out and say it. He wouldn't need a dinner to think it through and a walk on the beach. And anyway, this felt weightier than that. If she'd been the dramatic sort, she'd have described the atmosphere between them as momentous even. 'All right.'

He led her to a wide, spacious hammock that hung between two palm trees. She arranged herself at one end, he at the other. He rubbed his hands over his face and then gave himself a shake. 'Do you remember once asking me about my home life?' he said, his expression as serious as she'd ever seen it.

Ella's breath caught in her lungs. The question was wholly unexpected. What was going on? Was he actually going to talk to her? Now? Why? She didn't want that. Except, she did. God, she *did*. She wanted to know what made him tick. She craved information. So much so that she couldn't turn down this opportunity to get it. And so what if it did create some sort of a connection? It was hardly likely to be a deep one. They were already two-thirds of the way into their affair. In approximately a week's time, it would be over and all contact would be instantly severed, exactly as planned.

So she took a deep breath and said, 'How could I forget when you punished me so exquisitely for it?'

He gave her a fleeting smile that tugged briefly on

her heart strings and was gone all too soon. 'My upbringing wasn't very pleasant,' he said gruffly. 'Not
quite as tough as yours, but nevertheless, not very
pleasant. You said you'd read about my father.'

She nodded, thinking with an inward grimace of
the photos, the scandals and the lawsuits that had hit
the tabloids over the years.

'He was selfish and volatile. On occasion he could
be cruel. When he was around we walked on egg-
shells. When he wasn't, well, the press let us know
where he was and what he was doing. I can't remember a time when he wasn't having an affair. Sometimes
he brought the women he slept with home, which, even
at the age of six, I knew wasn't quite right.'

A wave of nausea rose up her throat and she swallowed it back down. 'How quickly you must have had
to grow up.'

'No quicker than you.'

Well, yes, that was true, but this wasn't about her.
'How did you all cope?'

'My mother dealt with it by moving to Northumberland shortly after Charley was born and hardly ever
left. When I was seven I went off to boarding school,
and once there, it was easy not to think about home
too much. As I got older, I stayed away as much as I
could. It wasn't hard. Whenever possible, I spent the
holidays with friends. When I wasn't doing that, I was
out. I partied hard. I screwed around. A lot. In fact,
some of my behaviour wasn't that dissimilar to my
father's. He once called me a chip off the old block,

and he was right. I didn't give a toss about anyone but myself, and I didn't care who I hurt in the process.'

Because it was too hard to think of the boy and teenager he'd been, adrift without support, having to rely totally on himself just as she had, Ella forced the image from her head. And because she didn't want to be feeling anything for him at all, she thought instead of the *Blush* magazine article she'd read and recalled how annoyed he'd seemed about it. 'You said that wasn't who you were any more.'

'That's right.'

'So, what changed?'

'My mother died. She took a fatal overdose fourteen years ago when I was eighteen and my sister was eight.'

When that information sank in, it immediately demolished her indifference. How terribly, terribly sad, she thought, her chest aching and her eyes pricking. How devastating that must have been. For all his material privilege, his environment had been just as traumatic as hers, although for very different reasons. 'I'm so sorry.'

'She was thoroughly miserable and by that point very fragile,' he said bleakly. 'But even so, it was my fault. She rang me that night. I didn't answer the call. If I had, I might have been able to save her.'

At the guilt in his voice and the torment on his face, the ache in her chest intensified. 'It wasn't your fault. It couldn't have been.'

'It was. I was out having too much fun. I was in

a nightclub at the time, with a girl, and I just didn't want to be bothered.'

'That must have been so difficult to bear,' she said, because who was she to try and convince him otherwise?

'It still is,' he said. 'But I'm trying to do something about it. You once asked me what was so important about Montague's.'

'You claimed it was all about the bottom line.'

'It's not about that. I want it back for her. While she was in Northumberland, she had an affair of her own. Just the one—with a neighbour. But my father found out. Ever the hypocrite, he took objection and retaliated. He knew Montague's meant a lot to her. Not because it was where they'd met—she as a trainee jewellery designer, he on tour of the company's North American assets—but because she'd been there since leaving school and had dreams of one day running the place. He sold it to Helberg out of spite, for a dollar.'

For a moment Ella didn't know what to say. Just when she thought Edward Courtney couldn't sink any lower in her estimation, he plumbed new depths. 'No wonder you want justice.'

Adam gave a nod and blew out a breath. 'Anyway, her death and my role in it was the wake-up call I needed. It made me reassess the way I was living. I gave up the hedonism and knuckled down. I finished university and then started working at the company back home. It was at that point that I realised how bad things were there. My father was CEO for nearly thirty years. In that time, he almost destroyed the business. When he died and I took over, I was determined to do things differently. I refuse to let his genes dominate me.'

'They don't and you have. You stopped the company from nosediving into oblivion, according to one press report I found. You turned it around in a year. That must have taken some doing.'

'It's taken sixteen-hour days, more often than not, seven days a week and a number of challenging personnel situations. But I wasn't having a company that was started by my great-great-great-grandfather vanish off the face of the earth while I was around to do something about it.'

Ella recognised his determination and ambition, and it occurred to her yet again that maybe they weren't that dissimilar after all. But that wasn't a particularly constructive thought, so she redirected her focus to his sister. 'How did Charley handle things?'

He frowned. Studied the sea beyond her right shoulder for a moment, then returned his gaze to hers. 'I don't know,' he admitted. 'I never asked. But she went through a wild patch as a teenager, so that could have been how.'

'I read up on Trouble Maker,' she said in case it helped. 'It seems to be doing well. Judging by the recent press it's had, it's heading straight for success.'

'So I've been told.'

'You sound as if you disapprove.'

'I don't. It's just…complicated.'

'In what way?'

'I don't really have a relationship with her, but I've found it hard to trust her nevertheless,' he said. 'She's made some bad decisions in the past. She quit school early and took up modelling. She got caught up in that world and went off the rails, and I'm pretty sure I don't know the half of what she got up to. That's why I made the trip to London that you questioned me about. She'd bought a flat. I was concerned it might be another bad decision. I didn't consider the implications of using the company jet at the time. I just wanted to get there as soon as possible. But when I did, she made it very clear that my concern was misplaced. And it was. The flat was fine. She had every right to be annoyed.'

In response to the flicker of discomfort that sped across his face, Ella felt her eyes narrow and her feathers ruffle. 'And was she?'

'Oh, yes.'

'Well, that's not fair,' she said, feeling quite outraged on his behalf. 'Presumably you have her best interests at heart.'

'I haven't always. I've let her down repeatedly. She once rang me, begging to come back home from the school our father had sent her to. I brushed her off. I wasn't there when she dropped out or when she got into trouble. I haven't taken the time to get to know her.'

'You weren't around. You were busy trying to sort out your father's mess.'

'It's no excuse.'

'Well, I think it is,' she said, bristling madly before thinking that she had to calm down. She really did.

She shouldn't be leaping to his defence. She shouldn't be feeling compassion and sympathy for him or dwelling on the lost boy and troubled teen he must have been. Even though she now understood that the reason he'd been so reluctant to answer her questions about Helberg and the flight to London back in the office was because both triggered deeply personal and evidently painful memories, it wasn't her responsibility to absolve him of the guilt he felt over his mother's suicide or his sister's troubled adolescence.

She must not get carried away. She must not read anything into what he'd told her at all. And why was he suddenly looking so intently at her? As if he wanted to devour her? Was the time for talking once again over? God, she hoped so, because she badly needed reminding that this was just sex. 'Why are you looking at me like that?'

'If I kissed you right now, would you assume I was trying to distract you?'

'Are you?'

'No.'

'Then what are you waiting for?'

Adam had never revealed to anyone what he'd just told Ella. In direct contrast to his father, he kept his private life private. He believed that enough of his family's dirty laundry had been washed in public and had always avoided personal interviews, partly because he feared giving up control of his narrative, partly because certainly in the early days of his stewardship of the company, he'd felt it would severely weaken his position. He'd certainly never been tempted to spill his guts to any of the women he dated, who'd never meant anything to him anyway.

So he hadn't known what to expect when he'd taken a seat in the hammock and begun to talk to Ella. Fire and brimstone? A crash of thunder or lightning strike? At the very least, he might have anticipated severe discomfort. Judgement and disapproval had not been off the cards either.

However, there'd been none of that. No rent heavens or plagues of locusts. She'd just listened, without prejudice. And the only moment of unease he'd experienced was when her eyes had filled with sympathy at his mother's suicide, which he did not deserve despite what she might claim.

Voicing it had been no worse than thinking it. In fact, he was more preoccupied with the outrage she'd displayed when they'd been talking about his visit to Charley. No one had ever come to his defence before. He'd always fought his battles on his own. He'd never had anyone in his corner. Yet in it she'd been.

His chest felt tight, his heart beating too fast. His head was spinning, even though he was half lying back. Above them, a vast canopy of stars twinkled in the inky blue night sky. Beyond the beach stretched the huge sea dotted with the odd light of a moored yacht. But all he was interested in was this hammock, which contained this woman. His gaze locked with hers. Her eyes were shining with invitation. A faint smile curved her mouth.

His pulse was thundering even before she removed her T-shirt, unclipped her bra and dropped both onto the sand. She shimmied out of her skirt and underwear until she was naked in the moonlight, and he thought he'd never seen such a beautiful sight.

'You're overdressed,' she said, her gaze slowly roaming over him and setting fire to his blood. 'I would help, but I wouldn't want to tip us onto the sand.'

It was a matter of moments to get out of the hammock, remove his clothes and apply protection, even though his hands seemed to be trembling. Then he climbed back in carefully and arranged himself on top of her, lowering his head to hers and kissing her until she was panting and moaning and the world around them disappeared.

Her hands were in his hair, on his shoulders, holding him to her as if not wanting to let him go. Carefully, smoothly, he manoeuvred her onto her side and wrapped himself around her, her back tight against his chest, their legs entwined. She twisted her head round and he kissed her again, one hand tangled in her hair, the other on her breast.

Desire poured through him. His heart was pounding so hard she had to be able to feel it. When he slid his hand down her body, she shivered and pressed herself against his erection, which ached and throbbed. His fingers parted her and she raised her leg to grant him better access. He found her warm and wet, and when she reached behind her to take him in her hand, he couldn't wait any longer. He held her hip, allowing her to guide him to her entrance, and when he was there, he surged into her slick velvety heat.

Ella gasped. His entire body shook. And then, cocooned in the hammock, so closely connected that not even the night's breeze could find its way between them, they began to rock together. Slowly, steadily, yet with an intensity that built and built and built, until she cried out softly and shattered, trembling against him as her fingers dug into his hip.

The powerful convulsions went on and on, clamping around him so relentlessly, so exquisitely, that they tipped him over the edge. With a hoarse groan, he pulled her against him and climaxed in a white-hot rush of ecstasy, pulsating into her harder and for longer than he ever had before, until he was limp, blitzed, completely hollowed out.

And just like that, he thought dazedly as they lay there, catching their breath, the sweat cooling on their bodies, the soul in the sex was back.

CHAPTER TWELVE

THE NIGHT ON the beach was something of a turning point as far as Ella was concerned. She had no idea why Adam had chosen to suddenly lower his guard after days of keeping it firmly in place, but she didn't much care. All that mattered was that this affair of theirs was now about as different to her last relationship as it was possible to get. There was balance. There was mutual respect and developing trust. There was also fun, because quite apart from the physical pleasure Adam continued to give her, he was also proving a most excellent host.

One afternoon he took her back up in the plane and patiently answered her *many* questions about the shipwreck, the islands, the resorts and the structure of a blue hole.

Another they went snorkelling, which was something she'd never tried before, European city breaks not really lending themselves to the activity. As impressive as the Caribbean was from the air, from beneath it was breathtaking. Just when she thought she saw the most beautiful creature on earth, along came another. Shoal after shoal of brightly coloured fish darted through coral the colour of amethyst, emerald, amber. A ray glided gracefully by not six feet away from her. One turtle that hung around for a while was half her size.

The following morning, Adam put her into one of the single sculls he kept in the boathouse, fitted himself into the other, and tried to teach her to row. Scything through the crystal-clear water, his upper body muscles rippling with every stroke he took, he made it look effortless.

It wasn't.

'Do you do this a lot?' she said, frustratingly unable to find any sort of co-ordination.

He rested his arms on his up-bent knees and watched as she went round and round in circles. 'I used to back in the UK. Now I have a machine in my apartment.'

'Handy.'

'In more ways than one.'

'What do you mean?'

'Lately, it's borne the brunt of my extreme sexual frustration. I must have rowed the length of the Mississippi since I met you. The morning after we first kissed, I completed ten thousand metres in thirty-nine minutes and twenty-four seconds. It was a personal best.'

Thirty-nine minutes and twenty-four seconds of bunching muscles and bronzed glistening skin? she thought, gritting her teeth as she accidentally loosened her grip on the oar and down went the blade. That, she'd liked to have seen.

'You just caught a crab. You won't make any progress if you don't concentrate.'

'Then you should put on a shirt.'

He just grinned, dazzlingly, at which point she promptly fell in. While she dashed water from her eyes, he paddled over. In revenge, she wobbled his scull until he toppled in too, a move she paid for with a long, hot kiss that had them dragging the boats up onto the sand, then rushing into the boathouse and tumbling onto a pile of tarpaulin.

Happily, conversation was no longer a one-way street, in either direction. There seemed to be nothing he didn't want to share with her. It was as if he'd kept everything bottled up for years, and now that he'd popped the cork he had no intention of sticking it back in. He told her more about his ancestry and his sister, with whom he was hoping for a better relationship. He detailed all the challenges he'd faced after taking over from his father, which sounded as though they'd been equally as tough careerwise as anything she'd undergone.

Because it was clearly a difficult subject for him, she didn't press him on his mother's death and the role he perceived he had in it, at least not initially. However, she became increasingly troubled not only by the thought that he blamed himself but also by the fact that he believed reacquiring Montague's would absolve him of his guilt.

She wasn't quite sure why she felt this way. She realised it wasn't up to her to persuade him to see the situation in any way other than his, yet she was filled with the urge to try, because for some reason it just didn't feel right. But how could she broach the subject? It wasn't something she could just drop into conversation, and it was the one topic he hadn't brought it up again.

The opportunity to do so arose the evening after the morning they'd spent rowing, when Adam took her by motorboat to a long curving beach on the northwest side of the island.

The sun had recently set and the darkening sky was streaked with orange, pink and red. As he switched off the engine and they glided through the shallows and onto the sand, she could see that a table had been set up beneath the spreading branches of what he had informed her as he'd driven her around the island a couple of days ago was a fofoti tree. It was draped with a white cloth, and on it were laid two places facing out to sea, complete with what she later discovered to be bone china crockery, polished silver cutlery and sparkling crystal glassware.

All around flickered dozens of candles and fairy lights wound through the branches above. To one side was a firepit in which bright flames danced. Two rows of tiki torches lined a path from the landing point to the table, and as he alighted to pull the boat farther up the shore, she thought that she'd never seen anything like it before. It was the sort of scene that sold holidays. It was the definition of paradise.

It was also extremely romantic, which meant she ought to be clambering back onboard and demanding he speed her back to the villa as fast as he possibly could, because what exactly was going on here? She wasn't remotely interested in romance. She'd always avoided it like the plague because raised hopes and false expectations would do no one any good.

But instead, her heart was racing, her throat was tight and she was thinking that, whatever the reason for this intimate dinner à deux, would it really be such a bad idea to enjoy it? She'd never been wined and dined by a gorgeous man who repeatedly rocked her world. She'd never been wined and dined at all. And how many hopes and false expectations could be raised in a paltry couple of hours when neither of them wanted anything more? None. So when Adam raised his arms to lift her off the boat, she willingly went into them.

'This must have taken a lot of effort to organise,' she said, her heart beating a little faster than normal once they'd walked between the torches and sat down at the table.

He reached into a cool box and extracted the ingredients for two piña coladas. 'Not particularly,' he said, mixing the drinks with impressive skill. 'We've exhausted the sights here, and I thought that since I couldn't take you to Aruba for fear of discovery, I'd transport Aruba to you.'

Determined to keep a lid on the wild tangle of emotions swirling through her, Ella swallowed hard and sought to keep things light. 'Is this how you seduce all the women you bring here? Because you needn't have bothered, you know. That horse has bolted.'

'I've never brought anyone here.'

She shot him a smile. 'Not even one of your many, *many* dates?'

He raised one dark eyebrow in her direction and handed her a glass. 'You read the article.'

'Along with half the female population of the country, it would seem.' She took a sip of her drink through the straw, the delicious flavours of rum, pineapple and coconut exploding on her tongue. 'I can see why you were concerned about the effect of all that gossip on your reputation and why you were so keen to stop it.'

'I couldn't take the risk of it upsetting the holders of the Helberg shares that I'll still need to acquire after taking Zane's and Cade's on Labor Day.'

This was the opening she'd been waiting for, she realised with a skip of her pulse. The chance to offer him a different version of events, perhaps. 'I know you're convinced that you'll win it,' she said, 'but what if reclaiming Montague's doesn't give you the absolution you're after?'

'It will,' he said, without even a second's hesitation. 'It has to. I've lived with the guilt of being responsible for my mother's suicide for fourteen years. It's crushing. It's stopping me from pursuing a relationship with Charley. This is my one shot at redemption. I'll never get another.'

'I'm not sure you even need it.'

Momentarily stunned into speechlessness, Adam set down his drink and stared at her as if she'd sprouted horns. 'Of course I need it. You even know why.'

'I think you're wrong,' she said, more certain of it than ever. 'I don't think you're responsible for anything at all. Obviously, no one knows the workings of your mother's mind at the time, but you said yourself that she was fragile. If she went to Northumberland straight after having Charley and left her behind in London, it's possible she may even have had postnatal depression.'

He sat back, his expression unreadable. 'What makes you the expert?'

Ella ignored the note of warning that tinged his voice because she was on a roll. 'Clearly, I'm not,' she said, wishing he'd give her a chance at least. 'Especially when it comes to maternal instincts. But that doesn't sound like normal behaviour. It sounds as though her marriage made her miserable right from the start. Do you know if she'd tried it before?'

'No.'

'So she might have done. She might also have called a dozen people before you who didn't pick up either. And even if you had saved her that time, she might have succeeded another. If what happened to her is anyone's fault, it's your father's. I really don't believe it's yours.'

'Well, I do.'

'I think it would help if you tried to let the guilt go.'

'I think we should agree to disagree and talk about something else.'

Adam got up to prod the fire, and the conversation did indeed turn to something else, because even she could see that she was banging her head against a brick wall. But it stayed with her nevertheless. Even though she thought him deluded, he was clearly tormented by what he believed to be the truth, and her heart continued to break for him. Whenever she remembered all he was doing to assuage his conscience, she couldn't help but worry. If only he'd take on board her points. But this was evidently a red line for him, and there was nothing more she could do.

It hadn't escaped her notice that since the night he'd decided to open up to her, she too had been experiencing a new dimension to their affair. Whenever she had a moment to herself, she kept replaying the intimacy of what had happened in the hammock after he'd finished talking. The minute she'd turned on her side and he'd wrapped himself around her, she hadn't just felt wanted. She'd also felt safe and protected, which was unexpected, because she was used to providing her own safety and protection. Even more bizarrely, she hadn't wanted to shake him and the feelings off. She'd wanted to pull him and them closer. Then, as they'd rocked together, slowly, steadily, her heart had swelled until it seemed too big for her chest.

But this didn't unduly trouble her. Nor did her

growing fascination with him or the connection that was developing. However great this affair was turning out to be, she wasn't remotely concerned that she wouldn't be able to walk away from at the end of it. Her promotion still flashed as bright and shiny as ever. Her career was still her number one priority. This was still just a celebration of her promotion and a bit of fun until real life called. And that was the way it would stay.

To Adam's gratification, opening up to Ella had been a truly excellent idea. She was no longer holding anything back. The tension had gone. The sex was even better than before. Their goals were once more re-aligned, the equilibrium restored, and it was all deeply satisfying.

They shared the values of hard work, determination and integrity. Right from the start, she'd kept him on his toes. And she seemed to get him—their difference of opinion about his role in his mother's death notwithstanding, because he would never agree that he wasn't at fault for that. His mother might have been suffering from depression. She might have called someone else that night who hadn't picked up either. She might have tried it before and maybe she would have tried again, even if he had saved her. He'd never know. All he had to go on were the facts, so he could never just 'let the guilt go' as Ella had suggested.

They even had the same approach to relationships,

as he discovered over a platter of lobster at lunch one day.

Having once done a course on dining etiquette which had covered crustacea in week three, Ella picked up a claw and carefully bent back the thumb to pull out the cartilage before cracking the shell and neatly extracting the flesh. He, on the other hand, simply twisted the body from the head and then bashed it with a hammer.

'That's what I'd quite like to do to my ex,' she mused as the shell shattered and he pulled it apart.

'So would I.'

'But then I only have myself to blame.'

'How?'

'It was my fault for reading more into the relationship than there was there. I completely forgot my rule to keep things casual.'

'Are you not a fan of commitment?' he asked, now applying the hammer to the claw in a move that would no doubt appal her course instructor.

'I've fought too hard for my independence to let myself rely on someone else, and I've worked way too hard to sacrifice everything I've achieved for the demands of a husband and kids. I have a plan to reach the top, and I won't let anything get in the way of that ever again. Not even myself.'

'That makes sense.'

'What's your excuse?'

Adam swapped the hammer for a fork and thought he couldn't even begin to answer a question like that.

How could he tell her that he was a control freak with a fear of his world disintegrating if he relaxed his iron grip on it? How could he explain that rampant desire and volatile emotions threatened that control, so it was easier and safer to steer well clear? He'd have to explain why he'd made an exception for her, and he definitely couldn't answer that, because he didn't know why.

'I just don't have the time,' he said instead with a nonchalant shrug. 'I have too many responsibilities as it is. There aren't enough hours in the day to maintain a relationship as well.'

That seemed to satisfy her, judging by the thoughtful tilt of her head and then the nod. 'Well, it's good to know that our expectations are the same.'

'It certainly is.'

The more time he spent in her company, the more he came to realise that he didn't just enjoy the sizzling chemistry that showed no sign of burning out—he liked her. A lot. He admired her willingness to give everything a go and then put one hundred percent effort into it. He could listen to her talk about herself for hours. He'd never thought of auditing as a particularly exciting field, but she did. Her face lit up when she expanded on the subject, and so suddenly and unexpectedly, he found it fascinating too. When she told him more about the trailer park, he wondered what his company did to help the disadvantaged in life and whether it could do more.

Their affair was soon coming to an end, and that

had always been the plan. But now he couldn't quite recall why. It felt wrong. He wasn't nearly done with her. She wasn't out of his system at all. His desire for her had not waned, and although their conversations had sometimes lasted long into the night, he was certain there was still much left to learn.

So, why couldn't they continue this back in New York? Not forever, of course, but perhaps until it petered out of its own accord. Night after night, he lost control with her and the world hadn't imploded. Indulging the still raging desire he had for her had led to no recklessness here, and he saw no reason why it should anywhere else. He didn't know what he'd been so afraid of. They had a good thing going, and it felt wrong to bring it to an unnatural close.

As he stood in the kitchen and fried up some plantain for breakfast, Adam wondered what Ella would think of that plan. If he'd read the situation correctly, he suspected her expectations might have moved in that direction too. Every now and then, he'd caught her looking at him in a way that suggested that she wasn't done with him either. He would ask her and find out. Once he'd answered this call.

In the back pocket of his shorts, his phone rang and vibrated. He turned off the gas and pulled it out. It was Maggie, his secretary, on the other end of the line, who he hadn't heard from since he'd left the city, other than receiving an email about some upcoming travel plans that he'd yet to open. Strange how all that seemed very far away.

'Good morning,' he said, and thinking that if Ella agreed to extend this affair of theirs, it could turn out to be a very good morning indeed.

'I apologise for disturbing you while you're on vacation,' said Maggie, sounding not quite as thrilled with the day as he was. 'And I hope you're having a lovely time. But I thought you'd like to know that I've been sent a photo by one of my contacts at *Blush* magazine. Of you and a woman who is not Annabel St James disembarking the plane in Aruba. It's due to go live on the website in an hour.'

Because his thoughts had been so wrapped up in other things, it took Adam a moment to process the information. Once he had, he went very still. His pulse spiked and his blood ran cold. White noise rushed through his head and his stomach heaved.

'Send it to me,' he said, his voice sounding to him as though it came from deep under water.

'I just have.'

Numbly he switched apps and opened up the picture. He and Ella were walking down the steps of the plane. They weren't touching. They weren't even looking at each other. But something about it nevertheless suggested intimacy. They were far too close to each other for him to ever be able to pass it off as anything professional. And there was no mistaking it was them. The focus was that sharp.

As the implications of what he was looking at sank in, an icy sweat coated his skin. His breath stuck in his lungs. He felt sick. Dizzy. As though he were about to pass out. With superhuman effort, he forced himself to exhale and get a grip. 'Put a stop to it.'

'It'll be pricey.'

'Whatever it takes.'

'Consider it done.'

He cut the call and put the phone down, and it was then that the numbness vanished and all hell let loose. His vision blurred and his heart crashed wildly against his ribs. The strength drained from his limbs, and he had to sit down before he collapsed. All he could think was that if this photo had appeared in the public domain and caught the eye of Cade and Zane he'd have lost Helberg in an instant. Montague's would have been gone. Redemption would have been history. Everything he'd been working so hard for recently, over.

How the hell could he have let it happen?

How could he have lost control of the situation so badly?

Because he'd been overwhelmed by chemistry so powerful he hadn't been able to resist its allure, that was how. Because he'd been arrogant and reckless in assuming he could have both Helberg and Ella. Because somehow he'd managed to forget that from the moment they'd met, the second their eyes had met in that bar, she'd repeatedly had him throwing caution to the wind.

At what point had he completely lost his mind?

What the hell had he been *thinking*?

This affair should *never* have happened, he thought, his breathing harsh and choppy. He should never have succumbed to temptation. Fourteen years ago, in the aftermath of his mother's death, he'd sworn to avoid the kind of desire that wreaked destruction and ruined lives, and he'd stuck by it. But he'd broken those rules, and bent many more for the sake of a fling with a woman who he'd even recognised was dangerous.

And as for extending it, was he mad? How would that even have worked? How had he thought they'd be able to continue seeing each other under the radar in a city of twenty million? Labor Day was still three weeks away. They'd have eventually been caught by *someone*. *Blush* magazine would have had a field day. To the world at large, he'd have cheated on Annabel and his reputation would have taken a huge hit, which would have displeased both his board members and the Helberg shareholders. And it wasn't as if he could have simply fixed up a three-way meeting between Annabel, Cade and Zane to clarify the situation. They'd never have let him get away with it, even if they had believed him.

The truth was, since he and Ella had arrived on this island, he'd barely given the bet a second thought. He'd barely given *anything* a second thought. His laptop had been gathering dust. He'd let numerous calls go to voicemail. For the first time ever, he'd put the executive team he'd created in charge, and he hadn't even wondered whether they were doing a good job of running the company in his absence. He'd been wholly wrapped up in Ella, in some sort of a make-believe bubble with her, so far from reality that they might as well be on another planet.

Well, that bubble had burst. Reality had stormed in like a horseman of the apocalypse, and here was the chaos he'd feared. He'd put a stop to this particular photo, but he couldn't risk another. He'd had a very close shave, and he wouldn't put in jeopardy everything he was trying to achieve again.

When he thought of Montague's in the hands of Zane or Cade, his heart practically stopped. If that happened, he'd never get justice. He'd be carrying the guilt he felt over his mother's death for the rest of his life. His sister would remain at a distance forever, and he simply couldn't allow it.

So forget how much he liked Ella. Forget the incredible sex and the appreciation he had for their conversations. She turned him into the man he'd fought hard to erase, the man he didn't wish—and could not—afford to be. She had to go, and she had to go for good.

CHAPTER THIRTEEN

ELLA WAS CLIMBING out of the pool when she saw Adam bearing down on her like a thunderstorm. What could possibly be wrong? she wondered with a frown as she picked up a towel and wrapped it round herself. She'd left him in bed, limp, sated, with a huge smile on his face, but that was nowhere to be seen now.

He came to an abrupt stop in front of her, the tension radiating off him in waves that were so huge she felt buffeted. His jaw was set and his face was as dark as night, and great big fat alarm bells started ringing in her head because, whatever it was, it had to be serious.

'I've just been sent a photo of us getting off the plane in Aruba,' he said grimly and without preamble. 'It was scheduled to appear in *Blush* magazine online. I don't know who took it, but there's enough detail to suggest that we're more than just colleagues. Take a look.'

He thrust the phone in her direction. Stunned, unable to quite comprehend what he was telling her, Ella took the device from him and glanced down, her mind instantly spooling back to nearly three weeks ago. She recalled the moment only too well. The two of them had just stepped out of the plane and onto the steps. A second earlier he'd reminded her of what he was planning to do to her when they got to the house, and she was wearing a secretive sort of a smile that somehow managed to imply that she couldn't wait to get her hands on him.

'How did this happen?' she said, her mouth dry, her heart thudding while she struggled to absorb its implications.

'I don't know, but I intend to find out,' he said with such icy steel that for a second, she felt sorry for the perpetrator. 'I've stopped it going public. However, it was an extremely close call. We got lucky this time, but I can't risk it happening again and putting into jeopardy everything I've worked for. You know what that means to me.'

'I do.'

'This island is not as safe as I assumed. We could be discovered any moment now.'

As that observation hit her brain, Ella's blood drained to her feet. No. God. That couldn't happen. What if her colleagues found out what she'd been doing? The gossip would be unbearable. They'd never trust her again. And if the picture reached her boss? She'd be fired in an instant, because an auditor and a client in cahoots on a Caribbean island the day after winding up a job was about as big a conflict of interest as there could be. The audit would have to be redone. Her reputation would be trashed. She really would never work again.

Despite the heat of the morning, a rash of goose bumps broke out all over her skin and she found she was trembling. All right, so Adam had blocked the photo's publication, but that wasn't the point. The point was that she too had jeopardised everything she'd worked for—not to mention the promotion she'd literally just received—and for what? Sex. A man. Again.

So, what the hell had she been thinking? How could she have let desire once more hurl her off her path? Hadn't she done enough damage to her career already? Had she learned *nothing*?

Ella had never regretted agreeing to this affair, but she did now. She regretted it with every fibre of her being. It had been a mistake from the start. She shouldn't have allowed Adam to persuade her into it. She should have been resolute. She couldn't *believe* she'd let history repeat itself, despite telling herself over and over again that it mustn't.

'You need to leave,' he said curtly, his voice slicing through the tumbling chaos in her head. 'Now.'

He was right. She did. She needed to find her things, pack up and get out of here as fast as she could. Back to the city, back to the plan, with her fingers crossed that this one photo was it. Once there, she would revert to eating, sleeping and breathing work. She wouldn't so much as *talk* to a man, let alone touch him, kiss him or lose her mind over him.

Yet, for some reason, she couldn't move. Her feet seemed to be rooted to the spot. She couldn't tear her gaze from his, and suddenly she was finding it almost impossible to breathe.

What was going on?

Why wasn't she moving?

Why was her chest so tight?

More pressingly, why was the realisation that leaving here would mean never seeing him again now the only thought in her head?

Surely that shouldn't matter. She'd been due to go home the day after tomorrow anyway, and she'd never had a problem with that. In fact, she'd relied on the time frame to keep her on the straight and narrow.

But it seemed it was a problem now because she didn't want to go. She wanted to stay here. With him. And not because she still had to get him out of her system but because she simply couldn't contemplate *not* staying.

Which meant what? she wondered, her head spinning and her stomach churning with confusion. That, despite her best efforts, she'd become emotionally involved with him? Well, she had. She'd known that days ago and had accepted it. Only she'd badly underestimated the effect it would have on her. She'd thought she'd be able to stay in control. But at some point she'd clearly lost it completely, and now she was in so deep she couldn't get out. Worst of all, she didn't *want* to get out.

The idea of leaving him cleaved her in two. It made

every cell of her body rise up with denial. Was she truly never going to be able to touch him again? To kiss him? To close her eyes and inhale him? It didn't seem fair. It made her heart physically hurt.

If she was being honest, these last few days, whenever she'd thought about returning home to the city she loved, alone, without him, her spirits had dipped. How would she fit back into her little life after this whirlwind of an experience? It was going to be like switching from Technicolor to black and white. Who would she talk to? Who would she laugh with?

And surely he couldn't *want* her to go. He seemed as invested in this as she was. Look at the steps he'd taken to get her here. The control he lost in her arms. He'd opened up to her. He'd given her Aruba. This was no more purely physical for him than it was for her, she was certain of it.

So maybe they didn't have to go nuclear.

Maybe there could be an alternative solution.

Straightening her spine and fighting the fog clouding her thoughts, Ella swallowed hard. She took a deep breath, summoned up every drop of courage she possessed and said, 'I agree that we've had a lucky escape. And I understand the need to leave. But what if this doesn't have to be the end?'

Adam went very still, not an inch of him moving, apart from the muscle that flickered in his cheek. 'It does,' he said flatly. 'You know why it does.'

'We could put this affair of ours on hold until Labor Day. You win the bet. I focus on my job and put some clear blue water between the audit and us. And then we start up again in September.'

He gave his head a sharp shake. 'It's out of the question.'

She frowned at the bluntness of his tone. Wasn't he overreacting? 'Why?'

'That was never the deal. We said three weeks.'

'I know. But am I out of your system? Because you're not out of mine.'

'You absolutely are. And there is no "us."'

Ella inwardly flinched, as if she'd received a thump to the gut. But she wasn't going to let this go when she believed him to be so wrong, when they didn't have to destroy something this good. 'Then, what have the last few days been about?'

'Sex.'

'Nothing more?'

'No. Why? What have they been about for you?'

Falling in love.

She stilled at the thought that darted through her head, and her whole body froze. No. That couldn't be right. She didn't want to be in love, ever. Look at what had happened the last time she'd tried it. Not that that had been love, she'd realised when she'd fallen out of it so swiftly. But the real thing would be even more unacceptably distracting. It would mean having to consider someone else's feelings and wishes. It would mean compromise, sacrifice and distraction. She'd never get to the top of her profession, ideally running one of the big four firms, without total single-mindedness. She couldn't think of anything worse than constantly battling for control of her career as her private life got increasingly complicated.

Yet, was love the extra dimension to the affair that she'd noticed following the night the hammock? The warm fuzzy feeling she'd developed? It could be. And when she thought about it, the rest of the evidence was pretty damning too. She adored sleeping with him. She couldn't get enough of his company and she was riveted by his conversation. The minute she was in his vicinity, every sense she possessed sharpened. He blew her away with his strength, his resolve and his determination to do the right thing. He made her feel safe and protected. He was steadfast and reliable. If she allowed him to, she had no doubt he would take on her ex and her firm, just as he'd been prepared to confront the lech in the bar who'd chatted her up the evening they'd met.

She'd always believed that she had to depend on herself and herself alone. She'd been let down so many times—by her parents, her employers, Drew—and had learned from an early age that she was her best and only champion. But she'd be able to depend on Adam. He would never let her down. He fought for the things he cared about, whether it was justice, his company or his sister. Would it really be such a bad thing to have him fight for her too? She'd been marching through life on her own for as long as she could remember, and it was exhausting. And lonely. So very, very lonely.

Perhaps she'd been ever so slightly overdramatic

with the whole must-stay-single thing. Perhaps the key lay in choosing a partner who had similar values and an identical work ethic to her own. Similar drive and ambition. Someone who would totally understand when she had to stay late or work weekends because they did that too.

Adam was that man. He wouldn't demand she make sacrifices to accommodate him. He wouldn't feel threatened by her need for independence. He operated entirely on his own too and he wasn't threatened by anything.

Okay, so he'd said he didn't have time for a relationship, but everyone made time for the things they wanted to do and people they wanted to be with. She just had to show him she was one such person. They could figure out the details later. They could be great together, a power couple taking the city by storm. She could have everything she hadn't even known she wanted.

'I've been falling in love with you,' she confessed giddily, her heart feeling too big for her chest, the wild jumble of emotions too great to contain.

Adam tensed and paled, which wasn't very encouraging. But he had a habit of backing off when she got too close for comfort and, as he'd discovered repeatedly over the last few weeks, she was extremely tenacious, so there was no way she wasn't going to add, 'And I think you've been falling in love with me.'

He flinched as though winded and took a step back.

He gave his head another sharp shake, his denial un-equivocal. 'You're mistaken.'

'Am I?' she said, the image of the future they could have together so dazzlingly brilliant that she could see nothing else. 'Do you talk about your mother with everyone? Do you resort to subterfuge and buy a pri-vate jet for all the women you sleep with? And what about the romantic dinner you arranged the night you brought Aruba to me? Is that standard practice?'

His body was now rigid with tension. His expres-sion turned even stonier. 'I warned you not to read more into this than there actually is, Ella.'

'I don't think I am.'

'It wouldn't be the first time you've made the mis-take of thinking yourself in love, would it?'

At that, the dazzling future vanished. Ella stifled a gasp and reeled, his callow observation shredding her heart to ribbons. She couldn't believe he'd said that. How dare he turn her confession on her like that? Who was this man? Where had the Adam of the past few days gone? How could she have forgotten how ruth-less he could be?

'That's a low blow,' she said hoarsely, her throat oddly tight. 'And this is quite different.'

'How?'

Well, quite. How? Her heart hammering, she men-tally sifted through the last three weeks, her temper-ature steadily rising when she realised that it *wasn't* different. He'd never promised her anything. She'd just assumed. She'd done what she'd sworn not to do. She hadn't kept it casual. She'd allowed her starry-eyed self to be swept off her feet and ended up far more invested in their affair than him. Just as she had before.

'Are you honestly saying you feel nothing for me?' she said, her head spinning with confusion and despair.

'That's exactly what I'm saying.'

For a moment, she couldn't breathe. The ground seemed to be shaking. She felt as though he'd reached in, pulled out her heart and then trampled all over it while she lay beside it, bleeding, dying.

But what could she do? She couldn't force him to feel the same way about her as she did about him. No amount of tenacity would make him love her. She wasn't wanted. And that meant she couldn't be here any more. There was only so much humiliation she could take. Only so long before her strength drained away and she collapsed into a soggy heap on the tiles.

So she lifted her chin and pulled her shoulders back, and before she lost what was left of her dignity, she said, 'I'll get packing right away.'

CHAPTER FOURTEEN

EMBARKING ON THE travel plans Maggie had discussed with him back in the office nearly six weeks ago and then followed up with an email he'd eventually opened once Ella had gone, Adam touched down in Rome first thing on Tuesday morning, certain he'd done the right thing in cutting off all prospects of a relationship with her and denying any feelings for her that he may or may not have had.

That photo had been far too close a call, he thought darkly as he listened to the plans for refurbishment outlined by the general manager of the seven-star hotel the Courtney Collection owned there. She was safe. As was he. They'd both had an incredibly lucky escape—for him that had been personal as well as professional—so he booted both her and their conversation firmly from his head with no regrets about any of it. He didn't miss her or wonder how her promotion was going. He didn't think of her and their three weeks together at all.

A week later, however, as he toured the factory in Hanoi, which manufactured leather goods for one of the businesses in the Collection, he had to admit he was struggling. Ella filtered into his head annoyingly often, and that scene by the pool kept nagging at his thoughts.

But he still held firm the belief that sending her home had been the best thing to do. He couldn't have agreed to a continuation of the affair from Labor Day onwards, even though he'd had to bite back the *Hell yes* that had been on the tip of his tongue. She'd still strip him of control and civility and tempt him into recklessness, and from there it would be a quick descent into chaos and destruction.

It was only natural to miss her, he reflected in between meetings that felt interminable. They'd packed a lot into three weeks. The memories would soon fade. And he'd eventually shake the image of her stricken face when he'd accused her of making a mistake about her feelings for him. He had not been proud of himself for that, but he'd had to get her away before he'd caved in and agreed to—and with—everything she'd said.

But by the time he arrived in the Blue Mountains wine region of New South Wales at the end of August, he was wondering what the hell he'd done. Every moment they'd spent together and every conversation they'd ever had were etched into his head. And now, as he sat in a presentation about the projections for next year's Shiraz sales, all he could think was, had he completely lost his mind? How could he ever have believed himself not in love with her? He was wild about her. He probably had been since the moment she'd dealt the jerk in the bar a knee in the groin and a martini down his shirt the night they'd met.

She was the only person who knew everything about him. She was the only person for whom he'd bought a private jet, resorted to subterfuge and arranged a romantic dinner. He thought she hung the moon and the stars. He worshipped the ground she walked on. She was magnificent.

She was also totally right about the hold that the past had on him.

En route from Hanoi, he'd happened upon an article in a magazine entirely dedicated to the green credentials of the Courtney Collection. The article was great—and so it should be when, where possible, he'd invested heavily in sustainable, ethical manufacturing and clean energy—but that wasn't the point. The point was that two months ago, not that he'd have known exactly who was writing the article, when it was to be published and in which publication, but he would also have demanded to see a copy before it went to print. This one, however, he hadn't even been aware of.

It had hit him, then, like a blow to the head, that he'd almost entirely stepped away from the company in order to focus on Ella and their affair. He'd ceded control and disaster hadn't struck. His recklessness had not led to chaos and devastation. Everything he'd worked for was still standing. He'd built something strong and lasting. Which proved he *wasn't* like his father in that respect, and perhaps not in any others either.

For years, he had feared that if he didn't keep a tight control on everything and everyone, the genes he shared with his father would overrun him, but although he looked like the man, he *wasn't* a chip off the old block. Yes, he'd once been selfish, thoughtless and irresponsible, but he'd been a teenager in a mess. Fourteen years had passed since then—years he'd spent knuckling down and forging his own path—and they counted.

The three weeks he'd spent away from the helm suggested that he didn't have to keep quite such an iron grip on everything as he'd always believed. He could afford to take his foot off the pedal from time to time. He could afford to let go.

And not just of his issues with his father. But of those with his mother too. Because he wasn't responsible for her death. Or maybe he was. Either way he'd never know.

Acquiring Montague's certainly wasn't going to give him any answers, he'd come to realise when he revisited the conversation he and Ella had had over piña coladas, awake and alone in the early hours in one hotel room or another. And it wasn't going to bring his mother back. How could it? And what if it didn't give him the absolution he craved? What if nothing would?

Did he really want to spend the rest of his life trapped in the past, hounded by his fears? Shouldn't he try and take a leaf out of Ella's book by accepting what had happened and moving on? If he just let it all go—as she'd suggested—he wouldn't need redemption. He'd be free. Free to explore a relationship with his sister. Free to look to ahead instead of behind. Free to have Ella in his life with all the challenge, excitement and love she would bring to it.

So the only question that remained was, would she feel the same way?

It didn't seem likely. When he thought of the manner in which he'd spoken to her, he felt physically sick. Driven by a ridiculous need to protect himself, he'd lashed out and hurt her. Devastatingly. He didn't think he'd ever forget the bewilderment and pain in her eyes when he'd dismissed her feelings for him and denied his for her. The memory of it tore him apart and brought him to his knees.

He had to fix the mess he'd made of things, he thought grimly and repeatedly on the twenty-hour flight back to New York. He missed her more than he'd ever imagined possible. She was the most incredible woman he'd ever met and he couldn't contemplate a future without her in it. He wanted her in his corner, in his bed, in his heart. He wanted everything she had to offer and give her everything he had in return. He would do whatever it took to get her back, he vowed above the Pacific, the southern states and then as they came into land. He just hoped he hadn't left it too late.

For the first few days that followed her return to the city, Ella kept herself so busy she barely had time to breathe. Focusing purely on the practicalities, she filled the fridge and did the laundry. She watered the plants, sorted her post and then started prepping to go back to work and take up her promotion.

She had no intention whatsoever of wasting any more time on Adam, she reminded herself firmly whenever she was unexpectedly hit by a memory of something they'd done together or a conversation they'd had. She had never shed tears over anyone, let alone a man, and she wasn't starting now. It was the super strong air conditioning that had stung her eyes on the long flight home, nothing else.

She wasn't some wilting Regency heroine, pining over an unrequited love. She wasn't a romantic any more than he was. She was a realist, a pragmatist, even if for those three crazy weeks, she'd temporarily forgotten that.

Every time she revisited that scene by the pool, which was far too often for comfort, she cringed. The things she'd said to him… The mortifying assumptions she'd made… The foolish feelings she'd thought she'd developed…

What on earth had she been *thinking*? she repeatedly wondered with incredulous despair. Where had that soppy, sentimental wreck of a woman come from? That wasn't her. That had *never* been her. Going all gooey at a few fairy lights and candles on the beach? Please. Fancying they shared some sort of an emotional connection? Honestly.

She simply couldn't fathom how she'd actually believed herself to be in love with the man when she'd known right from the start that it was nothing more than a fling and he'd made her no promises. And as for putting him on some sort of a pedestal, as if he were a paragon of strength and protection to be worshipped, well, who knew what that had been about? She must have entered a parallel universe for a while.

But she was back in the real world now, back on track, and she needed no further distraction. So with more effort than she'd have liked, she shoved Adam from her head and forced herself to look forward. Which worked. Mostly. Enough, at least, to mean that come Monday morning, she was cool, calm and raring to go.

This was the start of the rest of her life, she told herself as she leapt out of bed and into the shower and resolutely did not think about the many showers she'd shared with the man who'd turned out instead to be a paragon of disappointment. It was what the whole of the last twelve months had been about—the chance to put everything behind her and move on with rising to the top of the auditing world.

However, the minute she stepped across the threshold of the company that had been her spiritual home for the last three years, something felt wrong. She ascended the lift to her floor and headed to the new office she'd been given, but with oddly little enthusiasm.

Nothing about the building had changed. Her colleagues were perfectly pleasant, even congratulatory, which should have delighted her way more than it did. It was just that she had the bizarre feeling she wasn't the same woman who'd walked out the door six weeks ago.

Although supremely confident she could do the job, she felt off balance. For some reason, she was on edge. She couldn't seem to shake the conversation she'd had with Adam about the circumstances of her promotion. She was hounded by the voice in her head, which sounded annoyingly like his, demanding to know whether she was really okay working at a place that was prepared to treat her so badly.

Despite her best efforts to banish it, it stayed there, relentlessly hammering away at her and dredging up memories of horrible conversations with management, the same management who'd so recently authorised the promotion that should have been hers all along.

It took the shine off her new role. It made her question her judgement and kept her up at night, tearing her apart in the early hours because she'd fought so hard for it and wanted it for so long, yet now…she didn't. In fact, it gave her self-respect so much grief that in the end she had to resign, so yet again her career was disrupted because of a man she'd become involved with.

But even though it had been a tough call to make, the subsequent absence of angst absolutely confirmed that resigning had been the right thing to do. The company's values did not match her own, and hers mattered a lot. And at least this time, *she* was in control of the professional decision she'd taken. It was now five days since she'd quit—Labor Day, in fact, not that the date held any significance for her at all—and she already had half a dozen interviews lined up. She had no doubt she'd have her pick of offers. So it was all good. It was all very good indeed.

Of course, resigning and leaving the office immediately to work out her notice at home had meant that she now had a lot of time on her hands with nothing much to occupy her brain. Endless trips to the gym might exhaust her body, but her mind seemed to be on overdrive.

But if she caught herself increasingly dwelling on her secret Caribbean affair, well, why wouldn't she? It had been intense. She and Adam had packed a lot in. It was only natural that she experienced the odd moment of regret that he hadn't wanted to continue their relationship, because she did miss the sex. Who wouldn't?

She didn't miss him, though. Oh, no. These days, she barely ever thought of the conversations they'd had and the things they'd done. She was over him. They were done. She wasn't remotely interested in whether he'd won Helberg today and found the peace he sought.

And, yes, she might very occasionally have expended some energy reviewing how it had all ended, trying to figure out what had gone wrong, whether she could have done anything differently, but that was the analyst in her.

It would soon stop, she assured herself as she arrived back home after an hour on the treadmill. She was sure of it. At least she hoped it would. Because what choice did she have but to forget about him and forge ahead? It wasn't as if he was suddenly going to appear right in front of her and declare his undying love for her. Heaven forbid.

Keys in hand, determined to fill the rest of the holiday with something productive, whatever that might be, Ella stepped out of the lift onto the fourth floor of her building—and froze. Adam was pushing himself off the window sill outside her condo as if he'd been waiting for her, as if she'd conjured him up just by thinking about him.

Her heart stopped. Her breath caught in her throat. Her vision blurred and her head swam, and for a second, all those defences she'd built to protect herself trembled because it had been so damn long and she felt like someone dying of thirst coming face to face with a glass of water. But she kept them in place. She steeled herself to stay calm and held at bay the emotions she could feel trying to muscle their way in. She'd been vulnerable before him once and he'd crushed her. She would not allow that to happen again.

'What are you doing here?' she said coolly, noting that he looked tired and drawn but stamping out the urge to take him in her arms and smooth away the lines, because how he looked was none of her concern, and he didn't deserve her care anyway.

'I've been travelling,' he said gruffly. 'I came straight from the airport. Can we go inside?'

Absolutely not. She couldn't have him in her apartment. Even if she physically got him out, the memory of him in her space, space which she'd worked so hard for, would be unbearable. 'No.'

He frowned. Rubbed a hand across the back of his neck, then gave a short nod and cleared his throat. 'Right,' he said, shoving his hands into the pockets of his jeans and locking his gaze on hers. 'Then I'll just have to do this out here.'

She ignored the slow burn of heat that looking into his eyes always generated and lifted her chin. 'Do what?'

'How have you been?'

Was that why he'd come? To enquire into her wellbeing? Surely a phone call would have sufficed. Not that she'd have answered it. 'I could not have been better.'

'Promotion going well?'

'I resigned.'

He went very still. 'What did they do?'

'*They* did nothing. I just kept thinking about how they treated me and decided that it wasn't good enough. It was less than I deserve.'

'That was brave,' he said, a glimmer of what could have been admiration lighting the depths of his mesmerising blue eyes, although what did she care? It mattered not one little bit what he thought of her decision. 'I have contacts if you need them.'

'I have plenty of my own.'

'Of course you do.'

For a moment, he just looked at her intently, as if trying to get a glimpse into her soul. Her heart thudded heavily, and a flurry of jitters flitted around her stomach, which was not how she wanted to feel, so she blinked to break the connection and pulled her shoulders back. 'What do you want, Adam?'

He hauled one hand out of his pocket and shoved it through his hair. Then he took a deep breath and let it out slowly, and she might have thought he was nervous if how he was feeling was of any consequence, which it wasn't. 'First of all,' he said with another quick clear of his throat. 'I need to apologise for what I said to you by the pool just before you left the Caribbean. It was unacceptable and cruel. I was thrown off balance by the photo. It triggered a reaction I'm not proud of. I'm sorry.'

Ella's heart skipped a beat, but her guard remained up because an apology was the least he could give her. 'Don't worry about it,' she replied with a shrug that didn't feel quite as casual as it should. 'I was thrown off balance, too. We both said things we regret. Forget it. I have.'

He stilled. Frowned. A muscle jumped in his cheek. 'Have you?'

She gave a short nod. 'Oh, yes,' she said firmly. 'Totally. I really don't know what I was thinking. Perhaps I was suffering from sunstroke. Anyway, it's all water under the bridge, right?'

'No,' he said, taking a step towards her, a move that enveloped her in his scent and would have made her swoon if she'd let it. 'It's not all water under the bridge. And it's not right at all. Although you were. You were bang on. About everything. I *don't* buy private jets or arrange romantic dinners on the beach for anyone. I've *never* compromised my principles for an affair. I've only ever done those things for you. I am in love with you. I think I have been since the moment we met. You are the strongest, most incredible woman I've ever met. You frustrate me, you challenge me, you thrill me, and I want you in my life forever.'

Ella's heart crashed against her ribs and then began to gallop. But she must not weaken. She must not give rein to the emotions battering at her defences. She must not let him crush her again. 'Yet you hurt me,' she said, her voice nevertheless cracking. 'Badly. I told you I loved you and you denied it. You took something I told you, something personal, and turned it back on me.'

A flash of anguish sped across his face. 'I know,' he said, as earnest as she'd ever seen him. 'And I'm sorry. I was spooked and lashed out, and I deeply regret it. The thing is, Ella, ever since my mother died, I've feared losing control. I've always believed that without it, I'd cause the sort of chaos my father did. That night in the bar, you stripped me of it. I immediately reverted to type, acting without a thought for the consequences. You continued to remind me of the recklessness I am capable of, and I resisted that. The photo did too, and I reacted in the worst way possible.'

'So you got scared.'

He nodded. 'Yes.'

'That's no excuse.'

'I know,' he said, his tone filled with remorse. 'I have no excuse for any of it. But your take on my feelings for you wasn't the only thing you were right about. I've been doing a lot of thinking recently. And I've realised that I *do* need to let go of the control and the guilt that have kept me trapped in the past. I am not my father's son. I build things, not destroy them. And whatever my role in my mother's death, I'll never know for sure.'

His steady gaze continued to hold hers. 'I don't want to carry on living like this. I want to be free of it all. So this morning, I withdrew from the bet. I don't need Montague's. I don't need redemption any more. I don't need anything but you. If you'll have me. If I haven't screwed this up for good.' He stopped, his breathing a little shallow, a faint flush tingeing his cheekbones. 'Have I done that, Ella? Do you still love me? Or have I killed any feelings you had for me stone dead?'

Ella didn't know where to start with answering Adam's questions. She couldn't think straight. She was reeling. Struggling to process everything he'd just told her. He loved her? He'd listened to her? He was ready to move on and had given up Montague's?

As she stood there staring at him, her heart pounding so hard she felt as though it were trying to escape, one by one, her defences shattered. Every single lie she'd told herself vanished. And into the vacuum, every emotion she'd been battling to keep at bay flooded with the force of a tsunami.

God, she'd missed him, she thought, her chest aching, her throat tight. So very, very much. Despite her every effort, she hadn't been able to stop thinking about him. She'd been utterly miserable since she'd been back. And not because of the job, but because of him. Because he hadn't shared her hopes and dreams. Because she'd taken a risk and lost.

Returning to the city *had* been like switching from Technicolor to black and white. Everything had felt so flat. She missed feeling alive. Being kept on her toes. When she'd been struggling to work out what to do about her promotion, even though she was perfectly capable of making her own decisions, she'd wanted his advice and support. She'd had a glimpse of what a proper relationship could be like and to have it snatched away had been excruciating.

But now he was here, putting everything on the line, and perhaps she ought to make him pay for the agony he'd put her through, but it hadn't been deliberate. They'd both made mistakes. Neither of them was flawless.

'You haven't killed off anything,' she said, wondering if the floor beneath her feet was actually shaking or whether it was simply the force of the emotions swirling around inside her. 'I do still love you. But I'm not entirely happy about it. You crushed me. You sent me away. You've caused me nearly a month of misery.'

He closed the distance between them and took her hands in his. 'If you'll let me,' he said, tightening his hold on her as if he wanted to never let her go, 'I'll spend the rest of my life making it up to you. You're not the only one who's tenacious, Ella. I will do everything in my power to prove how sorry I am and how much I love you. I will fight for you and I will not fail. I will date you. I will woo you. I will bombard you with texts filled with heart emojis and emails laden with innuendo. You'll have to give in eventually, if only to get some peace.'

Her heart pounding, Ella gazed up into his eyes, which were filled with sincerity, determination and the steadfastness that she loved so much, and the last of her resistance melted clean away. Who knew what the future would hold? she thought a little giddily as happiness began to spread through her, warming every inch of her as it went. There'd be much to discuss. Much to sort out. But they'd both taken giant steps into the unknown recently—him relinquishing Montague's, her quitting her job—and so maybe now was the time to take another one. Because she loved him and he loved her, and the one thing she did know was that life with him would never be boring.

'Well then,' she said, her smile wide and bright and filled with everything she was feeling as she drew him with her towards her front door, 'you'd better come in.'

EPILOGUE

Fourteen months later

STANDING IN THE centre of the ground floor of the newly refurbished Montague's, listening to the hubbub going on around her, Ella couldn't remember the last time she'd felt so nervous.

Three hundred guests were in attendance at this launch party, and she'd spoken with many of them, but she could not recall a word of their conversations. She felt as though she'd drunk a dozen glasses of champagne instead of just the one. Her stomach seemed to be on a spin cycle.

She glanced around for the man of the hour and spotted him by the jewellery case that contained a million-dollar diamond necklace and matching earrings. At the sight of him, in a black dinner suit that emphasised his dark good looks, her heart turned over as it always did.

They'd come a long way since the Labor Day Adam had stepped into her condo and started the rest of their lives together with a kiss that she could still recall. With his support and advice, she'd decided not to take up any of the many job offers she'd received and to set up her own business instead. Now she employed two other auditors, and in time she hoped to expand her workforce and maybe, just maybe, even add a crèche.

True to his word, Adam had dated her and wooed her, even though she'd repeatedly told him that he didn't need to, because she'd actually forgiven him the moment he'd explained why he'd fought his feelings. He'd loosened his grip on the company and it was flourishing. He'd also let go of the guilt, and, free of the cage the past had trapped him in for so long, he'd pursued a relationship with his sister, which had gone from strength to strength.

When Montague's had become available, Ella had encouraged him to take it. He'd said he didn't need it, but because she'd thought he might nevertheless regret it later, she'd prevailed, and it had not escaped her notice that he'd taken more than a casual interest in the relaunch.

Once in his possession, he'd begun to raid it for gifts. A tennis bracelet here, a pair of diamond stud earrings there. Not an engagement ring, however. He'd broached the subject of formalising their relationship a mere three months into it, but she'd been a little more circumspect. It had felt too soon. He'd never given her any reason to doubt his commitment, and she knew he loved her, but she'd spent over a decade fretting about compromise and sacrifice and her independence, and old habits died hard.

However, a lot had happened since then. Six months ago, he'd persuaded her to move in with him, which had been a major step for her. But as it had turned out, compromise and sacrifice weren't a problem at all when the person you were accommodating was doing the same for you. Independence didn't disappear just because someone else's wishes became as important as your own.

And so now she was going to take an even bigger one.

'I need you for a moment,' she murmured when he reached her side, drawing him behind a pillar and away from the throng, her heart practically in her throat.

'That's something I'll never tire of hearing,' he said warmly, gazing into her eyes and smiling.

'I love you.'

'I love you too. More and more each day. Body, heart and soul.'

'That's how I feel,' she said, her voice a little shaky. 'I love how I can depend on you. I love how you lean on me. You make me feel protected and secure and at the same time, as if I can take on the world. I never thought I could ever have this. I thought I was destined to be alone for the rest of my life. You've made me happier than I ever believed possible.'

'Right back at you.'

'So I have a question.'

'What is it?'

She took a deep breath. Then she got down on one knee and held up a band of platinum. 'Will you marry me?'

* * * * *

Did Boss with Benefits *leave you wanting more?*

Then you're bound to love the first instalment
in the Billion-Dollar Bet trilogy!
Billion-Dollar Dating Game
by Natalie Anderson

And don't miss these other Lucy King stories!

Undone by Her Ultra-Rich Boss
Stranded with My Forbidden Billionaire
Virgin's Night with the Greek
A Christmas Consequence for the Greek
The Flaw in His Rio Revenge

Available now!

HARLEQUIN
Reader Service

Enjoyed your book?

Try the perfect subscription for Romance readers and get more great books like this delivered right to your door.

See why over 10+ million readers have tried Harlequin Reader Service.

Start with a Free Welcome Collection with free books and a gift—valued over $20.

Choose any series in print or ebook. See website for details and order today:

TryReaderService.com/subscriptions